SEX AND DEATH
IN TELEVISION TOWN

Sex and Death in Television Town

Carlton Mellick III

Eraserhead Press
Portland, OR

ERASERHEAD PRESS
205 NE BRYANT
PORTLAND, OR 97211

WWW.ERASERHEADPRESS.COM

ISBN: 0-9762498-5-5

Copyright © 2005 by Carlton Mellick III
Cover/interior art copyright © 2005 by Ed Mironiuk
www.edmironiuk.com

Printed in the USA.

AUTHOR'S NOTE

I grew up in a smallish town in the middle of the desert. It was basically just a suburb twenty minutes outside of the Phoenix metropolitan area, but the people living there didn't think of it as a suburb. They liked to pretend it was the Old West, and they were cowboys. These were the adults. The children were busy pretending to be transformers and thunder cats, and could care less about cowboys. The parents tried to get us to embrace the history of the area, but we wouldn't have anything to do with it, no matter how many times they took us to the Rawhide amusement park, fed us ranch-style beans, and got our pictures taken in sepia wearing Old West costumes. Unless they gave cowboys laser swords we weren't interested.

I ended up getting into the Western genre years later, once I was introduced to the Italian westerns such as the Django series. There's just something about Italian westerns that kick ass. Not as much as Italian horror movies, but pretty damn close. It was enough to get me inspired to write this Bizarro western, which seems to have turned out to be more like "Hell Comes to Frog Town" than anything else. But hey, that movie starred Rowdy Roddy Piper and he's a damn fine actor. Didn't you see "They Live?"

You better have . . .

- Carlton Mellick III 12/13/05 5:28 a.m.

THE JOURNEY TO
TELEVISION TOWN

CHAPTER ONE

The dildo is alive. She struggles with it, fights it, a penis-sized millipede squirming between her legs.

"You can fuck it too," she says, red-worming eyes at the young man sitting next to her. The woman: wiry nakedness, snakeskin pattern tattooed from neck to feet, enormous spikes down her spine like a metal stegosaurus.

She has to curl forward to keep her stegosaurus-spikes from cutting the upholstery. Eyes glued to the boy. A tongue like red soup.

There are six people crammed inside of this stagecoach. All on high nerves. Hot sweat in the air, sticky-stuffed together and this spiky snake woman keeps masturbating against them.

The young man: Random is his name. Maybe twenty years old, but with a ten-year-old's face. His head knotty with tension. His mouth wide open but there aren't any words.

He can feel the strange woman's naked skin next to him, through his red velvet tuxedo. She vibrates against his body, steel moans from her reptilian throat, curly insect legs inside of her.

His eyes diverting . . . Tries not to look, but she is

slipping her violent flesh in and out of his mind.

"They are getting closer," says a man with a green-painted face, cleaning his pistols and distant-eyed out of the stagecoach window.

Random refuses to look out of the windows. He can hear things out there. Things screaming and clawing in the distance. He can imagine them all over the landscape, scurrying through the black smoke. It is bad enough to see them in his mind.

But the worst image his eyes are avoiding is seated across from him: Typi, his young bride, who is soggy and skeletal and makes him cringe.

He remembers the sweet-sweet sixteen-year-old she used to be just yesterday morning, before all this happened, with her rainbow smiles and sunshine-colored hair. But now: puffy wrinkles, red bugged eyes, dreadlocked hair, her once-beautiful white wedding dress ripped into shreds and stained with mud and gore. She is frozen in her seat. Her brain completely numb to her new husband, to the people who saved her life. She doesn't even realize the woman masturbating next to her.

So Random focuses on his folding hands, rapidly folding and unfolding and wet.

He has not met any of these people before tonight, but he has heard rumors of them. He knows that most of them are part of the vicious Crawler Gang. A group of renegade hermaphrodites that have been terrorizing innocent farmers and councilmen, wreaking havoc from the silver coast to the end of the world.

Battle Johnny: (sitting next to Random's wife) The leader of the hermaphrodite gang. He looks only like a man and not at all like a woman, though he has the sex organs of both genders. His breasts are barely visible through his boiled leather vest.

The occupants of this stagecoach are all that's left of the Crawler Gang. And all that's left of the citizens of Jackson City.

"How many?" Battle Johnny asks the green-faced man.

"I can see a dozen or so. Might be more behind them." The masturbating woman gyrates faster. Excited with the gurgle-screams behind them.

A voice from on top of the stagecoach: "Which way?"

Battle Johnny's stern-grizzled face at the spiky woman.

"Almost . . ." the woman's mouth bulging, furious strokes with the metal millipede, until she explodes into orgasm. Her legs stretch tight against Battle Johnny's lap, fingernails digging into Random's thigh and squeezing the shoulder of the thin girlish person seated on the other side of her.

All her muscles are going loose and she drops her eyes shut.

Battle Johnny grips her kneecaps. "Which way?"

The woman grunts. She squirts the wiry insect out of her and then, with a wink to Random: cups her fingers, digs deep inside, and swirls out a handful of ejaculate.

She brings the palm of goop to her face. Her eyes roll, flutter, as she brings the scent of her sex deep into her lungs, and goes into a trance.

"What is she doing?" asks the green-faced man.

Battle Johnny raises an angry finger at him.

She drifts and sways. Dips her tongue into the slime and explores.

The desert makes black earwig sounds.

The woman opens her eyelids and with a butterfly voice she says, ". . . Telos."

The passengers jerk, her words like electricity jolting through their laps. One of them drops a gun.

"Telos?" Battle Johnny asks her. "Are you insane?" She wipes her goo across Random's red-velvet thigh. "Telos."

Voice on the roof: "Where to?"

Battle Johnny stretches his rubbery neck out the window. "Maulatin," he says.

"Maulatin, fine," says the voice on the roof.

"I said Telos!" the woman screams.

Battle Johnny leans back, shakes his head. "The people in Telos are unpredictable. There's got to be another place."

"You don't know what you're doing," she says. "There is no other way."

"I am like God," Battle Johnny says.

CHAPTER TWO

These are the characters:

1) **Random** – A random young man.

2) **Typi** – A typical young woman.

3) **Battle Johnny** – leader of the hermaphrodite gang.

4) **Nixx** – face painted green.

5) **Cry** (a.k.a. Sex) – Reason for their survival #1.

6) **Jesus** (a.k.a. Death) – Reason for their survival #2.

7) **Sharp** – a girlish hermaphrodite.

8) **Oxy** – a masculine hermaphrodite.

CHAPTER THREE

When they get to Maulatin it is in splinters, as dead as the past six towns. Riddled with skinless corpses and shredded buildings.

Everyone jumps out of the stagecoach and darts to the fallen citizens, rummaging through their guts for extra guns and ammunition.

Typi will not leave the stagecoach, her face white with sweat. Ghostly skeleton in a bride's gown.

"The horses are exhausted," someone shouts. "They need to be replaced."

Random steps out of the stagecoach and wanders through sticky dirt. Hermaphrodites run around with lanterns getting food, supplies, hoping they don't run into anymore survivors who need to be saved. They can't spare anymore weight.

The naked spiky woman finds clothes on a dead sheriff and tears off bloody strips of black fabric. She dresses — just barely, you can still see most of her breasts and crotch — by attaching pieces of cloth to hooks on her body.

She licks her tattood hands with a long snake tongue and sharpens her teeth on a stone.

"I told you there's nothing here," she says to Battle Johnny. "We need to go to Telos."

"Cry," Battle Johnny stomps on pieces of regurgitated human flesh at the half-naked woman, "I have been to Telos and I tell you it is not the right place."

Cry says, "They will help us. You know how to communicate with them. You can explain our situation."

Battle Johnny kicks a slimy skull across the dirt road. "You don't understand."

"We don't have a choice," the green-faced man says to them. "The only city left between here and the end of the world is Telos. There isn't anywhere else we can go."

"You don't know that for sure," Battle Johnny says. "Nobody has ever reached the end of the world."

Nixx, the green-faced man, shakes his head and returns to scavenging.

"You don't take my vision seriously," Cry says. "Why did you bother busting me out of jail?"

Battle Johnny raises his finger at her and then trudges through dead cowboys to the saloon.

CHAPTER FOUR

Random is sitting on the ground with opal-button eyes. The girlish hermaphrodite wipes bush thorns from her buttocks and sits down next to him. She is like a thin awkward teenager. Her head is smooth bald but peppered with white scars. Small round glasses. Painted-on eyebrows.

She looks at Random and says, "I was born backwards."

Random squints at her, then goes back to counting cactus shadows along the landscape.

"They call me Sharp," the girlish hermaphrodite says.

She is both a man and a woman but since she is very girlish they address her as *she*. Just as they address Battle Johnny and the stagecoach driver, Oxy, as *he*, because they are both very masculine hermaphrodites.

"We need to get moving," says Oxy with red-scraggle sideburns, leaving the stables with bags of horse food.

His accent is cruel and every word sounds like sarcasm. Random cringes when the man gleefully says, "Well, we're fucked. There aren't any living horses 'round here and my boys are ready to collapse."

Random never saw the two people riding on top of the stagecoach until now. He was in such a hurry to save his life, and the life of his catatonic bride who has been in a state ever since she saw her father's rib cage torn from his torso.

But now he sees Oxy with his vulgar chin and scrotumy hair. And he sees the other man standing on top of the stagecoach, his back facing Random.

A shadow of a man who can melt into the background like silence. Black trench coat blowing in the steel-flavored breeze. His head shifting slowly, eyes moving along the eastern horizon. It is moonless black that way.

Random looks to the west. Still a line of twilight in that direction. That is where Random wants to be.

"They call him Jesus Christ," the girlish hermaphrodite says about the shadow/stranger.

"Jesus Christ?" Random asks. "Why?"

"He can work miracles with bullets," Sharp says.

She raises her six-shooter with an awkward grip and tries to twirl the handle like an expert gunslinger, but it slips out of her fingers and thuds the ground.

She leaves it there. Pretends it didn't happen. "He says his real name is Death. He says he is the Grim Reaper."

Sharp stands up, brushes thorns and dirt from her pants.

"Is he human?" Random asks.

The black gunslinger drops from the stagecoach, out of sight.

"No," Sharp shakes her head. "He's something better."

CHAPTER FIVE

Jesus Christ can sense something.

He steps through needle bushes and scorpion pits, and peers deep into the darkness. The landscape is alive with movement and metallic sounds.

Dragonfly skin creeping the dirt.

He can sense hundreds of teethy jaws clattering in unison, razor claws slicing through the air.

"Let's go," Battle Johnny calls, stepping out of the saloon with a jug of the local whiskey. "Let's get out of this dump."

Jesus squints his pinhole eyes and spits tobacco on a dog's corpse.

Random hustles to the coach and tries not to look at his wife as he gets in. He sits next to her so that he can hold her hand, so that he doesn't have to sit across from her and look into her fear-webbed face.

Everyone is inside now but Death, who stands out in the desert watching the darkness.

Battle Johnny calls out, "Come on, time to go."

Jesus just stands there like a piece of the landscape.

"Let's go!" Battle Johnny screams.

Still standing there.

"Come on!"

Jesus goes "Shhhhhh!" and so Battle Johnny raises a finger at him.

One more squint of his eyes and Jesus is satisfied. He returns to the coach and takes his place next to Oxy, takes one of the shotguns from the pile on the roof.

"They're coming," he mutters to the side-burned hermaphrodite.

Oxy taps the brim of Death's hat and chuckles. "Maybe they'll catch us this time," he says, missing teeth, and whips at the horses "YAA!" back on the road heading west.

CHAPTER SIX

"She must be in another place," the green-faced man says about Typi, looking through her ear to see what's in her mind.

"She's ruined," Random says. "She became mine just today and already she's junk."

He bites his lip.

There are screeching voices in the background. Crawly things making their way closer to the stagecoach.

"The horses are slowing down," Cry says.

They look out of the window and see the landscape moving at a relaxing pace.

"Get those horses going!" Battle Johnny screams at the people on the roof.

Oxy calls down to them, "They're exhausted. If I push them any harder they're going to collapse."

Random can hear him giggling.

Battle Johnny raises his finger at everyone in the stage-coach and shuts his eyes tight, trying to think.

The others watch him, blocking out the scratchy-gurgle sounds coming closer-closer. And then he stops thinking and snaps his fingers at the people to his right.

"Nixx, Cry, get on the roof," he says. "Sharp, have your pistols ready. Make every bullet count."

Battle Johnny looks at Random who is trying to shake

life back into his bride.

"Boy, what's your name?" he asks him.

"Rrr-andom," he tells the hermaphrodite gunslinger. "Random." He nods at him and pats his shoulder awkwardly. "Do you know how to use *this*, Random?" He shows a bloody pistol to the boy.

Random shakes his head.

"Take it anyway," Battle Johnny says, poking its handle into his chest. "Don't use it unless one of them comes close to you. Shoot at point-blank range and you won't waste any bullets."

Random shrugs at the hermaphrodite. He takes the gun only to see if Typi will get mad. She does not approve of weapons, just like her father. She made him promise never to touch them, that she would rip out his eyes if he ever fired one shot, even at the ground. But she doesn't seem to notice the gun, still shivering, deep in stare. He wipes the blood off the shaft with her wedding dress, her mother's beautiful heirloom wedding dress. But no response. He points it at her head, between her eyes. No response. It is like he isn't even there.

Cry and Nixx climb up to the roof, balancing on spare guns and supplies, surrounded by violent whispers, growls and gnashing sounds from the shadowy parts of the desert.

"We're going to have to fight them," Cry tells Death, but he is already pointing his shotgun at things behind them.

Cry squats down and arches her back until it is C-shaped. The metal stegosaurus-spikes make crystal-ring noises in the wind and reflect lantern light into Nixx's eyes. He sees her as walking cutlery, a sadistic flesh-machine of erotic knives and razorblade kisses.

She sees Nixx admiring her figure and pinches his long ears.

"Can you really see the future?" he asks her.

She smiles and bites her puffy lower lip.

"Fuck me and I can make *you* see the future too," she says, waving her tongue at him like a river snake.

CHAPTER SEVEN

A horn blows from the southeast. "What is that?" Sharp asks, trying to get a good look out of the stagecoach window. Random listens for it, but won't look out the window. The horn blows again. A steam whistle. "It's a train," Battle Johnny says. "It's a goddamned train."

Random can hear the chug-chugging of a train in the distance, growing louder.

Battle Johnny thinks for a minute . . . "There's no towns southeast of here," he says. "Where the hell is that thing coming from?"

"And where is it going?" Sharp adds.

Battle Johnny has his finger raised, just slightly and none of the others inside the coach seem to notice, his mind whipping an idea into shape.

"Oxy," he yells out of the window. "Catch that train. We're getting out of this death box."

"The horses can't run anymore," Oxy yells. "We'll never make it."

Oxy combs his sideburns with rage.

"Force them to run," Battle Johnny shouts. "We only need them as far as the train."

Oxy doesn't respond, attacking his fiery hair with the tin comb.

"You got me?" Battle Johnny shouts.

Oxy stabs himself in the leg. Then grunts. "Yeah, whatever."

"Are you sure you know what you're doing?" Sharp asks Battle Johnny.

Battle Johnny cracks his knuckles at her. "We're lucky I'm the one in charge," he replies.

Sharp pauses at him. She drops her guns and kisses him deeply, wraps her wrist tight against the back of his neck and pulls his tongue into her mouth.

They speak to each other with eyes and the interweaving of their bodies. Words have never been an adequate expression for them. They are only lovers when there is silence.

The banshee-screams outside become like white noise.

CHAPTER EIGHT

The train churgles into view:

"That's no train . . ." Nixx says.

It is like a train, but it's something alive. A giant caterpillar-shaped steam engine crawling up the track. Decorated with bones and shiny black insect shells, greasy liquid draining from pores and leaving a wet trail across the landscape.

Oxy chuckles at it.

The meaty machine moves fast and squishy, red-gargles when the whistle blows, bubbling a rotten odor.

From behind:

Metallic squeals from pickled throats as the creatures emerge from the darkness. Buzzy rabbit-hopping creatures that move so twisty-fast that they are hard to make out.

"Christ," Nixx mutters as the desert below them fills with the crispy insect-things.

Battle Johnny raises his guns and screams, "Go for the train, the train!"

Random grabs Battle Johnny by the wrist, pulling his gun out of the window. He can feel water droplets slipping down his itchy cheeks.

"Wait, we can't go on *that*," Random cries. "It might be full of those things!"

Battle Johnny tears out of the young man's grip and

spits at him.

"The entire desert is full of those things," he says.

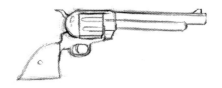

CHAPTER NINE

The stagecoach races along the train track. The horses gallop wildly, finding a second wind. They don't even need Oxy's whips of encouragement. The train gets to them before the creatures do.

Battle Johnny sends Cry to the caterpillar/train first.

"How do we get in?" Nixx asks Cry.

There aren't any openings.

The steam engine is close enough to touch. They can smell its thick meaty aroma misting from its sweaty exterior. It really is something alive. A flexing of fatty tissue as it chug-churgles beside them.

Cry smooths her muscles and pulls a handleless samurai blade from beneath her thigh skin.

"We'll make an entrance," she says.

With cat-like movements, Cry slashes the caterpillar/train, cutting into its warm flesh. Black blood oozes out of the wound, soaks her fists and runs down her snakeskin tattoos. She licks her fingers and slashes again.

Down below, Random is twitching at the window. Hugging his knees and making sure he is sitting in the exact center of the coach, away from both windows.

"Why aren't you firing yet?" he cries to Battle Johnny.

"They're not close enough to aim," Battle Johnny says.

"What do you mean?" Random screams. "They're at our heels!"

Battle Johnny grinds his teeth. He tries to aim at the shifty black creatures but they are too fast. They run from side-to-side, spiraling, twisting from one place to another.

"Not close enough," he grumbles.

Above, Nixx has eight guns lined up evenly by his legs. They are all exactly two inches apart, four inches from his knees, and centered. The two rifles are in the middle. Three pistols are on each side of the rifles, placed according to size. All barrels of the guns face east, in the direction of the black creatures, except the two tiny pistols on each end which face west just in case one of those things tries to sneak up behind him.

The gnarling beasts are very close now, almost within shooting range. But Nixx isn't ready to ruin his gun setup.

Maybe when they get a little closer, he thinks.

So Nixx turns his attention to the woman next to him, who whimpers as she slices into caterpillar fat. He notices one of her hands on her upper thigh, squeezing fingernails tight into her tattoos as she opens up the train.

"Hurry up," Oxy says. "I don't know how long the horses can keep this speed."

Cry is masturbating now. Ripping into herself as she digs through the blubbery wall.

The hole is big enough to climb through, but Cry is too electrified to stop. She hacks at the sausagey meat violently, trying to bring herself to orgasm.

"Get in there!" shouts Battle Johnny's head, poking out of the stagecoach window at her.

She wheezes. Doesn't speak. Still masturbating as she climbs up the train's meat and slips down into the hole. Disappearing inside of the monstrous insect.

Nixx suddenly feels alone. The thrashing black things are closer, fizzling around the coach. Just below him. And he's supposed to be holding them off.

"What's in there?" he screams at the hole.

He doesn't see Cry. It is hollow and quiet inside.

"Is it safe?"

Nothing. Empty.

Just a gooey hole staring back at him.

CHAPTER TEN

"You go next," Battle Johnny yells to Nixx.

Nixx stares at his organized gun display and wonders if he should start using some of them. He can feel the warmth radiating out of the train's hole. It beckons him, the comfortable moisture, a vagina opening its lips to him.

"Hurry up, hurry up." Oxy rips at his sideburns madly.

The green-faced man ruins his gun display by taking the three shiniest pistols, and stuffs them in his belt. He quickly fixes the remaining ones into a pattern that is tolerable enough. And slowly reaches out for the edges of the hole, squishes fingers into the meat and leaps away from the stagecoach. His body presses against the sweaty caterpillar machine. Oil soaks through his shirt.

One hand after another, he pulls himself inside, careful not to lose his grip on the slippery flesh.

The last thing Nixx sees before going in is a blistery figure crawling up the back of the stagecoach.

CHAPTER ELEVEN

The interior:
    Nixx gets to his feet and whips a pistol out of his belt with artistic perfection. He holds it at a 45 degree angle (his mental compass tells him it is exactly 45 degrees) and scans the area for Cry.
    No sign of Cry.
    He is in a dark and wet place. Empty and loud with chur-churgle sounds.
    It is light enough to realize he is in some kind of passenger car, full of seats made of bloody rib cages but nobody to sit in them.
    "Cry?" Nixx calls, he can hardly breathe in this steamy thickness.
    Fluids dribble from tiny holes in the ceiling.
    Crying . . .
    Nixx hears whining, slippery cunt sounds. He steps through fishy blood puddles to a mohawk of spikes peaking out from behind one of the morbid passenger seats.
    "Cry," he says, relaxing the angle of his arm by 10 degrees.
    She is squatting in a pool of slime, fucking some kind of leg bone turned dildo. Wrapped up in the blanket-like shadows. Her claws extend from her fingers, she curls her body

outward and sniffs the air in Nixx's direction.

CHAPTER TWELVE

Outside:

Jesus Christ is standing on top of the stagecoach, calm and balanced, easing bullets into the twisty forms that charge the coach. He shows no emotion, uses no energy. Just empties his guns into black bodies like he's dealing cards in a poker game.

Crusty skulls explode into smoke as they reach the back of the stagecoach. Bullets rip through them like paper. They are hollow inside, and full of ash.

One leaps at the stagecoach door and shrieks its pimpled face through the window at Typi. Her eyes flicker at it until she comes out of her trance and finds herself screaming back at the wailing figure.

"Get out of the way," Battle Johnny yells as he pulls the girl to the floor and fires a bullet into its skull.

The creature explodes into clouds of soot, coating everyone in a layer of charcoal.

Typi hugs Random's feet, cries, drools all over his shoes. Random flicks his fingers at her.

"You two go next," Battle Johnny says to the young couple. He spit-cleans black dust from Sharp's glasses.

Random doesn't move.

"Get the hell up there," Battle Johnny says.

Random blinks rapidly. "But I don't think . . ."

Battle Johnny raises his finger at Random.

The young man flinches, as if the hermaphrodite was about to slap him instead of raise a finger. He helps his wife off of the ground and sits her on the seat across from him. He examines her with squinty eyes.

"Are you okay?" He pets the dirt-curls of her hair.

The girl explores him. She half-smiles and kisses his hand.

"Don't leave me," she cries.

He shakes his head and scrunches the plumpness of her shoulder.

"Get going," Battle Johnny croaks.

Sharp boosts Random up first, who stumbles, climbs up sloppily, and roll-bashes into Death's thigh. The gunslinger doesn't move. His legs are rooted to the coach's roof like nails. He doesn't even look at the young man as he pollutes the desert with black corpses and dust.

Typi comes up easier. She is very light, even for a sixteen-year-old. And though lacking in muscles, Random effortlessly pulls her to the top.

The girl bends to her knees, curling up into a safe ball. She rubs her bloody bare feet and gazes out at the landscape full of devils.

"What are they?" she asks.

Random is busy looking for the hole in the train.

"I used to have nightmares about this," Typi says to Death, her tiny kitten face looking up at him.

Death glares down, only for a second, long enough for his white pinhole eyes to pierce through her, molest her.

"We're slowing down," Oxy says. He chuckles under his breath. "The horses are losing steam."

Random sighs through his eyes as the train's hole drifts

farther and farther from his reach.

CHAPTER THIRTEEN

Below:

Sharp and Battle Johnny are holding each other again. They breathe each other's breaths and drink from each other's lips.

"Up," Battle Johnny says.

Sharp kisses him one more time then slithers out of the window and onto the roof.

She sees Oxy trying to drive the horses faster. He whips them, throws empty whiskey bottles at them, but he can't seem to get them going again. He is full of giggles while whipping the horses, excited by the futility of his actions.

"What are we going to do?" asks Random, folded over Typi's body.

Jesus Christ's arm twists backwards, popping out of joint, and three shots are fired at the ground near the horses' feet. They go from trotting to galloping speed. A crack-snapping noise when Jesus adjusts his arm back into its socket.

"Get ready," Sharp tells the couple.

She puts her hand on Typi's delicate back. "We might only have one more shot at this."

CHAPTER FOURTEEN

Oxy gets them back to the hole in the train.

"Bring the supplies with you," he shrieks to the girlish hermaphrodite.

Sharp and Random don't waste a second. They grab all the equipment stacked up on the stagecoach and toss it through the opening. They are both awkward people and not at all skilled at throwing items into holes. So much of their belongings thump against the side of the train and scatter across the landscape.

Sharp goes first. She doesn't even warn Random that she's going and leaps at the train, crawls up into meaty darkness.

Random turns around and Sharp's gone. His nerves crawl up his spine imagining one of those things ripping her off of the roof in a single stroke. He looks at Jesus for answers, but the gun-slinging messiah is busy working shotgun miracles.

"Come on," Sharp says from the train, waving at the young man.

Random oozes some relief and goes to Typi, still curled up next to Death. He pats her back, caresses her on the clean part of her wedding dress.

She quivers at him and rubs her cheek against his ankle,

purrs.

"I want to wait here for a little while," she says.

Random shakes her and whines something incoherent.

"You go," Typi says. "I'll be right behind you."

Random doesn't know how to argue with her. He buttons his collar and tucks in his shirt, then takes a running jump at the train. Sharp catches him by the wrists, helps him in. The pretty young man nearly collapses from the smell. His red velvet tuxedo is instantly covered in a smelly slime.

He goes back to the opening.

"T-typ-Typi," he calls out, but she is still scrunched up in a ball and isn't moving.

Death looks down on her with a crude frown.

"Am I a pretty bride?" she asks the man/shadow.

He goes back to firing his rifles.

"Girls are supposed to be their prettiest on their wedding day." Her voice sweet and distant. "That's what momma said. She woke me up at the crack of dawn so she'd have plenty of time to pretty me up for my wedding day."

"Get up here," Sharp screams.

"It was such a nice morning." She smiles and twirls a lock of blood-caked hair. "Momma and I wasted most of the time chatting. We just talked and talked. About when she was a young woman and how she met Pa. About her wedding day. About what I'll be doing on my wedding night."

Random squeezes the rim of the flesh train, screaming, but Typi's off in her own world.

She continues, "Momma wants to make sure I'm gonna have kids right away. I keep trying to tell her that Random isn't ready to be a father but she says," impersonating her mother's voice, "never mind you that, just get yourself pregnant. Don't give him a choice. Trick him if you have to. The boy'll have nine months to get himself ready. That's all a man needs."

Jesus stops firing and leans down to the young girl. He places a black-gloved finger over her scabby lips and goes, "Huusshhhhhhh."

Oxy screams out with cackles, hooting and yelping with amusement. "Here it comes," he cries.

Jesus looks up to see a horde of black creatures coming in from the north, cutting them off up ahead.

Oxy is hollering with glee, whipping the horses so that he'll get to the demons even sooner. "Faster, faster!"

The black creatures wait, ready to spring.

Just a few more seconds before they converge . . .

CHAPTER FIFTEEN

Oxy shrugs. He steps out of the driver's seat and dives smiling with gooey sideburns as he twists into the train's slit.

The horses barrel out of control toward the devil creatures, some trying to break free of the coach. Death doesn't have time to grab the reins. He picks up the young woman and throws her out of the way, at the train, and Random somehow catches her.

Two black widow six-shooters slip from Death's trench coat sleeves into his palms. His arms outstretched and ready for impact.

Random has Typi by the wrists, just barely. She is dangling in the air, screaming at him, kicking her legs. She can't get inside. Her bare feet try to push off against the side of the train but it's too slippery. Thick grease collects between her toes. And Random can't get a good grip on her with all her thrashing.

The stagecoach hits the horde of creatures with such an impact that it flips into a violent tumble.

Death is sent flying through the air.

He is still calm. He glides like a hawk over the deformed army, shooting them as he flies. The bullets from his black widows are composed of jade and onyx. They make plastic-hum noises as they shower from the heavens onto the rancid creatures below.

The horses wail as the demons graze into them, shredding their flesh with electric blender mouths. Random diverts his eyes from the horses, trying to block out their high-pitched squeals.

He doesn't yet realize that his young bride has been cut in half.

CHAPTER SIXTEEN

Random notices that Typi is suddenly lighter for some reason and can probably be lifted into the train now. When he looks down at her body, his jaw goes slack.

Everything below her waist is missing, her insides spilling out all over the desert. He sees her blood splattered against the side of the caterpillar train, mashed pieces of her legs clinging to the wheels.

And she is still alive.

She is still clinging onto Random's wrists, trying to pull herself through the hole.

Random cries out. He just watches as the halved teenager struggles in her wedding dress, blood exploding out of her mouth.

"Randi . . ." she wheezes at him.

An intestine is uncoiling rapidly out of her torso like rubber yarn, leaving a trail that stretches all the way back to the stagecoach wreckage.

She pulls herself up to the edge of the hole, looking Random in the eyes. He smiles at her. He doesn't know what else to do.

The pain is like millions of wasps. She can feel every inch of her intestine lying across the desert. There must be half a mile of it now. She can even feel all the way back to the stagecoach as something begins to gnaw on her intestine with metal teeth.

Typi wraps a convulsing arm around her groom's neck and pulls herself up to his face.

"Forever," she whispers into his lips.

Her eyes close and she kisses him, slides her tongue and large globs of blood down his throat. Random doesn't know how to stop her.

Before she is finished, her body goes limp. Her tongue droops to the side of his mouth.

Random doesn't move. He lets her body fall away from him, drop off the train into a puddle of mud.

All he can think about as her half a body becomes a part of the distance is how her wedding dress no longer looks anything like a wedding dress.

CHAPTER SEVENTEEN

Battle Johnny wakes up.

He is inside the overturned stagecoach, looking up through the window at the stars.

The screech-burble noises are surrounding him, scraping against the wood of the coach, and he realizes that he is alone.

His pants have been torn from his lower legs, blood painted so that he can't see his leg hairs, but nothing's broken.

He peeps out: It is dark around him. He can barely make out the back of the train as it moves away from him in the distance. Hundreds of devils chasing the rear.

There aren't too many of them left here. Only about a dozen or so. He can see the outlines of their little childlike bodies. They are squatting down, tearing the horses into strips and rubbing the blood on their necks and potbellies. They are so engrossed in the strips of meat that they don't even bother killing two horses that are still attached to the coach.

Battle Johnny feels for his pistol but the holster is empty. He looks down, too dark, he feels the floor for a gun. Fingers crawling like tarantulas. There is a corpse here. His hand stumbles into it and bursts through the skull, gushing into a pouch of chalky dust.

Examining the body with his fingers: the skin is as hard as wood but thin. And it is hollow inside. Its internal organs are made of dust.

His hand digs deep inside.

"There's got to be something inside of them . . ." he whispers to the body. "A heart, a stomach, something . . ." No hope for him to save his life so at least he can satisfy a curiosity.

Burrowing through crumbly innards, Battle Johnny hits something halfway through the body, at the point where the chest meets the stomach. It is something solid and cold. Something metal.

Battle Johnny grabs it with two fingers and pulls it out of the dust.

"A gun," he says, rubbing his palm against.

It is a strange shape for a gun, long fat barrel and most of it is coated in fur, but still a gun.

Without giving it a thinking, Battle Johnny takes a knife from his boot and climbs out of the stagecoach. The creatures shriek at him as he thuds onto the ground and fires at them.

At first he thinks the gun doesn't work because the bullets don't make any noise. They shoot like tiny arrows. The only noise is the cutting of air.

The demon children scatter and Battle Johnny charges to the horses. His legs must be hurt worse than he realized because he has a severe limp and isn't going very fast.

A shrieking black shape skids in front of him and cuts open his chest. Then disappears before Battle Johnny gets a chance to shoot. Another strikes his back and he cries out. He turns to it, but it is already gone.

When he gets to the horses he notices that they are not actually all that alive. One has a spear of wood stuck in its neck and the other has a large wound on its stomach.

He chooses the one with the stomach wound, cuts it from its harness and mounts it. Then off he goes. Riding bare-backed on an injured horse.

CHAPTER EIGHTEEN

Death is on top of the train, near the ass, bouncing on a mound of plump flesh. With his black widows, he shoots spider-shaped bullets into black figures crawling up the sides of the train.

Coming up the tracks, he sees Battle Johnny in the middle of the demon horde, whirling a strange furry gun over his head, riding a horse with its stomach dangling inside-out. The creatures rip into him as he goes, slicing off strips of his skin, a bit here and there, but they can't get him off the horse.

Death climbs down the back of the train, waiting to help him out if he makes it that far. If there's anything left of him by the time he gets there.

Battle Johnny takes the pain like a man, as if he isn't part woman at all. And he makes it all the way up to the back of the train before the horse starts to stumble over its own guts.

CHAPTER NINETEEN

Cry and Nixx are naked together. Wrapped up in a sweaty pool. She has him pinned down underneath her crotch. Her giant metal spikes pointing at the ceiling, gyrating as she stretches him out. Mouths full of the taste of each other.

Across from them, the others have set up a lantern but there isn't very much light. They can just barely make out each other's curvature in the red-flickering.

"What do you see?" Cry asks as she finishes coming into the man's mouth.

He can't speak. Her vagina muscles are tight around his tongue and don't want to let him go.

The other people are disgusted with them, pacing up and down the aisle, blabbing "How can they do that at a time like this?" and "What the hell is wrong with them?"

Cry slicks her glossy stomach down his face and rests her chin on his chest. Smiling into him and waiting for an answer.

"I see people with strange heads," Nixx says.

The woman puppy-licks him. "Telos."

"How do you do that?" he asks.

"My cum is magic," she says. "I have a wizard for a cunt."

And she pets her pubic hair at him.

"Where did you come from?" Nixx asks.

She blinks at him and laughs. "I like you, you look like an elf," and pinches him on the nose.

Nixx lays his head into a pillow of meat and imagines windmill blades on the ceiling.

Cry wipes her fingernail across the goop on Nixx's lower lip and sucks it into her mouth.

Her eyes drift and roll for a moment.

"We're headed there," she says.

Nixx raises an eyebrow.

"This train is going to Telos."

CHAPTER TWENTY

"I hate it when I'm alive," Random says, sitting on a rib cage chair full of lungs that breathe against his back. His heart pounding out of his fingertips.

The air is hot and thick.

Sharp and Oxy are ignoring him, sitting by the train hole pointing guns, not bothering to comfort him even though they know that's what he wants. After Typi died, they shrugged at Random and figured that was enough.

Their guns almost go off as a door opens up out of the meat next to them, strings of tissue extend as Death and a staggering Battle Johnny enter the car covered in soot and blood.

Sharp leaps to her feet and goes to Battle Johnny. Cry and Nixx are re-clothed and go to the hermaphrodite to figure out why he is still alive.

Battle Johnny holds up the furry gun. It is not at all like a gun. More like a sculpture made of squirrel-hair, rat tails, and plastic dolls.

"Where did you get it?" Nixx asks.

"Inside one of those things," he says. "It saved my life."

Battle Johnny hands him the gun and walks away from them. Barging through Oxy's shoulder. Not in the mood to discuss anything right now. His wounds are deep and he's beginning to feel dizzy, itchy-brained. Just wants to sit down and rest for a bit.

Sharp goes to him. She wraps her arms around him and he kind of hugs her back. He slumps against her shoulder.

"Battle Johnny?" she says.

She looks him in the eyes and sees tiny black hairs wiring out of his face. No, they are like veins, something underneath his skin.

Nixx pulls Sharp away as he sees what is happening to the hermaphrodite. There is something seriously wrong.

Battle Johnny falls to the floor, a high-pitched squeal echoes out of him as his face begins changing. His flesh blackens, his eyes lose color.

Sharp breaks away from Nixx and drops to Battle Johnny. But before she reaches him, a blade chops off the top of his head.

The girlish hermaphrodite bird-screams as a bowl of her lover's skull falls into her lap. Full of a fizzing charcoal-coated brain. Inside the rest of his head, he is also infested with sizzling black meat, some kind of chemical turning his insides into ash.

Cry crouches down over Battle Johnny and examines the opening she made. The fizzling slows and then stops.

"It's a plague," she says.

The others jump back, including Sharp who flings the skull cap and cries into her fist.

"Get him out of here," Jesus says.

But the others just stand there, watching the half-blackened man like television.

CHAPTER TWENTY-ONE

There is a long period of silence.

Sharp sits next to Random in the quiet place. Oxy is asleep on a giant liver and Death is exploring the rest of the train.

Cry and Nixx are back on the floor where they were having sex. The green-faced man thinks he has some personal connection to her since they have fucked and has been following her around the train like a stray cat.

"What do you think it will be like in Telos?" Nixx asks her.

She scratches him behind one of his elf-like ears. "I don't know."

"You can see the future," Nixx points at her vagina. "What is going to happen to us?"

"I can't control my sight," Cry says. "I just see random images of the future in my sex."

"Tell me if you ever see me die, okay?" Nixx says.

"Are you sure you want to know?"

"Positive."

"Why?"

"I want to prepare myself."

"That's all?"

"I want to go out with a bang."

She rolls her eyes at him. "I don't think you really want to know."

"I'm not joking."

Her fingers curl around his elfish ears.

"I've already seen you die," she says.

Nixx slaps her hand away from his face. "You lie. You're just teasing."

Her face is sincere.

"I saw your death back on the stagecoach," she says. "That's why I slept with you here. I thought we might not have another chance to fuck before you get killed."

Nixx shakes his head at her. He doesn't want to believe her but can't think of anything to say.

"I like to fuck every person I come across," she says. "Too bad I didn't get a chance to experience the young bride. She was a sweet little girl."

Cry gives Nixx a glassy smile and rubs her scaly green legs.

Death returns.

He tells them, "No one on the train."

"Impossible," Cry says. "Who's driving it?"

"No driver," he says. "Just empty cars like this."

Cry pushes Nixx away from her. "We're heading for Telos," she says.

Death nods his head.

Cry curls up into a sleeping position on the floor. "It's possible the train is a living creature." She sighs at the men and hermaphrodites. "Guess it can be driving itself."

The shadowy gunslinger walks away from them and out of the boxcar.

"Strange guy," Nixx says.

"He's just a baby," Cry says, closing her eyes on his green-painted face.

CHAPTER TWENTY-TWO

In the morning, it is like none of this ever happened. The sky is turquoise blue with billowy clouds over the desert. Prickle-green bushes and cacti and chirping yellow birds.

Random leans out of the hole in the train to inhale the painting. There aren't any creatures anymore, no dead bodies, no sign of destruction. The young man absorbs the sunshine and pretends he's not on such a horror of a train. Watches the wrens hopping across limbs of Joshua trees.

"It's not over yet," Cry says to him from under his feet. He doesn't know how long she's been there.

The train goes underground and comes back out. Random wonders if there are creatures hiding under the ground.

This is all that they have left:

1 broken lantern
1 tin of mackerel
½ jug of whiskey
2 shotguns with 1 shell each
8 pistols with 3/5/1/1/6/3/2/2 bullets
1 furry alien pistol with ? bullets
1 Hoak bow and 8 arrows (Nixx's)
7 random bullets

2 black widow pistols with 3 bullets each (Death's)
1 blade from a samurai sword, missing a handle (Cry's)
1 shotgun, empty
17 pistols, empty
1 hunting knife
1 wood-cutting axe
1 gold wedding band (Random's)
2 bags of miscellaneous clothes, mostly socks
1 jar of green face paint (Nixx's)
assortment of crudely-designed dildos (Cry's)
1 pair of eyeglasses (Sharp's)
some rotting fruit
1 loaf of molding bread
the clothes on their backs

Cry also has many items attached to her that should go into their inventory but she claims they are parts of her and not items she carries.

Nixx demands to be the organizer of their equipment.

He puts it all in a neat circle around him and makes piles. He creates a garbage pile and discards the empty guns, the rotten food, the whiskey, and the lantern into it. Oxy steals the jug of whiskey and drinks it in front of him.

"Not a good idea," Nixx says to Oxy but doesn't try to stop him from drinking it. And Oxy doesn't stop drinking it.

Then Nixx empties all the guns and piles the bullets together. There are 30 bullets. He makes five piles of bullets with six bullets in each pile. Then he places one gun on each of the five piles and discards the other three. He loads one shotgun with both shotgun shells and discards the other.

Sharp kneels to help Nixx load all the pistols but he slaps at her hand and shoos her away.

Oxy takes the bad fruit and bread from the garbage

pile and has a snack.

"That's it, that's all of it?" Random asks, eyeing the bullet piles.

Nixx nods and makes six piles for each of them:

Oxy: shotgun with 2 shells, axe, 1 pistol with 6 bullets
Cry: dildos, blade, furry gun
Sharp: 1 pistol with 6 bullets, eyeglasses
Nixx: Hoak bow with 8 arrows, 1 pistol with 6 bullets, green face paint, gold wedding band
Death: 2 black widow pistols with 3 bullets each, 2 regular pistols with 6 bullets each
Random: 1 hunting knife

Oxy adds the whiskey and old food to his pile.

They share the tin of fish for breakfast and change their socks.

Cry gives Random the furry gun. She says, "I don't use them." And takes the knife away from him. He doesn't seem to care either way. He doesn't make a fuss about not getting a gun in the first place. He doesn't make a fuss when Nixx takes his wedding ring either, even though it's the closest thing the group has to money.

"Six strangers," Sharp says.

The others look at her.

"All of our friends and family are dead," she says. "We're stuck with each other. All strangers."

"What about him?" Nixx points at Oxy. "Isn't he part of your gang?"

"I barely know him," she says. "He didn't mix well with us."

Oxy chokes on his whiskey.

"I fucking hate hermaphrodites," he says, rubbing his tits at them.

Cry stands up and stretches her spiky parts. "Well, we're stuck together. From now on, we're all family."

Family. Random thinks about that for a while. Death is like a father and Cry is like some kind of child-molesting mother. With children in descending order of maturity: Nixx, Sharp, Oxy, and finally himself. He guesses Battle Johnny would have been the oldest sibling and Typi the youngest. But they are gone now. Only the crazy middle children remain.

Random decides to remember Typi as a younger sister. It's easier for him this way.

CHAPTER TWENTY-THREE

The train goes underground again but doesn't come back out.

They are in the dark for nearly half an hour before they realize that it's not coming out again.

"What's going on?" Nixx asks Cry.

The underground brightens but they are still beneath the Earth. Iridescent light emanates from the walls here.

Random looks out of the hole. "The lights . . " he says. "Like the light of the moon."

"This is our stop," Cry says as the train slows and gargle-whistles.

It stops in a wide-open area, still deep under the ground.

They just stand there, in the train. There aren't any people around. Anywhere. The train sits, huffing and bubbling. No passengers getting on or getting off.

"Come on," Cry says to them as she climbs out of the hole. Death follows after her.

The four children hesitate to leave, but eventually decide they'll be much safer with mommy and daddy, and pile out of the meaty hole. Random exits last.

Outside of the train, they stand there and look around. They are in an enormous subway. The ceiling is dozens of feet high. The iridescent lights make Random dizzy.

The train's whistle blows and it chargle-chugs slowly

away, into the dark unlit parts of the underground.

They are all alone. Their eyes shifting every which way but there is nothing much to see. Just a wide cavern with smooth walls.

The sweaty parts of them begin to freeze.

"Where is it going?" Random asks, about the train. His voice echoes.

"There's nothing that way," Oxy says. "Any farther west and it'll fall off the end of the world."

"The track probably twists north or south," Nixx says.

"Or maybe the end of the world is its destination," says Sharp.

Cry waves their questions away and calls them useless.

She points to a tall iron ladder that goes up a few dozen feet and then disappears into the ceiling.

"Must be the way out," she says.

Before anyone can argue, Jesus begins climbing the ladder. They have no choice but to follow their protector.

ARRIVAL IN
TELEVISION TOWN

CHAPTER ONE

The six strangers arrive in Telos through a manhole.

"It is just like home," Random says.

The town does resemble Random's home town, Jackson. But most cities look like Jackson. A typical Old West town. Full of wooded patchwork buildings.

"Where are they?" Nixx asks.

"Are they all dead?" Random asks.

"It's still early," Cry says. "Nobody's awake yet."

But then they see one of them, over by the general store: A stocky man wearing overalls and a box on his head, sweeping mud off the porch.

The six of them approach the man and notice he doesn't have a box on his head. His head is just box-shaped. It is a television/head. Right now, some nature channel is on. A show about a zebra drinking from a meadow.

"What is it?" Sharp asks.

"One of *them*," Oxy says. "A bastard Telosian."

"What the hell is wrong with his head?"

The television man faces them and adjusts the volume dial so that the strangers can hear the television show more clearly. He just stands there, facing them.

The narrator of the nature program is discussing the lifestyle of the zebra. None of these strangers have ever seen a zebra before, though Random has seen one in a picture book. It amazes him to see one come to life inside of this Telosian's head.

The television man turns the knob on his cheek and his face changes from a nature show to an infomercial on some kind of cooking doodad. He waves his hand inside of his shop, trying to lure them in with a dirty finger.

"What is that?" Sharp asks about the kitchen utensil. "Why did his face change like that?"

"I think that's their language," Oxy says.

The six of them walk on and the shop keeper tries to clamper after but his face starts to go a bit fuzzy. He adjusts the long metal antennas on his head until the picture is clear, then continues sweeping his porch.

CHAPTER TWO

"What do we do?" Random asks. "Are we safe here?"

"The goblins won't attack Telos unless they know we're here," Cry says.

"Do they know we're here?" Sharp asks.

"Probably," Cry responds.

Walking the dirt road to the center of town, only the saloon seems alive. People still awake from all-night drinking.

A television man tumbles out of the saloon, rolling off of the porch backwards and he lands in the dirt. Out steps another television man with fancy black and white clothes. Standing tall and elbows out like bat wings. His antennas like devil horns.

The tall Telosian's face is playing a silent vampire movie. The one on the ground is playing a family sitcom.

Random sits down in the soil and watches the sitcom. Right now there are some wacky neighbors coming over to visit some mischievous kids and a dog tracking mud onto the carpeting.

The sitcom Telosian gets to his feet and zigzags his arms desperately at the other. Random tries to watch the sitcom but the screen keeps moving around frantic.

The silent horror movie television man walks slowly

to the twitchy one. He draws his gun. No, it is not a gun but a remote control. He points it at the sitcom face and fires. It doesn't kill him. Just changes the channel.

The sitcom face tumbles back. The show changes from the family sitcom to another sitcom with zany cross-dressing roommates. The sitcom face struggles to reclaim balance. But the horror face fires again and the roommate sitcom becomes a sitcom with kooky black people that tell jokes about being black people. Fires again. Another sitcom, one with screwball policemen hitting somebody on the forehead.

The sitcom face rolls back. Another shot fired. His face now a sitcom with babies talking.

The horror face then rapid fires his remote. The sitcom face flying all over like bullets are splashing blood from his body.

His face changing to more and more sitcoms:

Another wacky family sitcom, a redneck family sitcom, an office sitcom, a bar sitcom, a black people family sitcom, a rich white people family sitcom, a sitcom about a family who is supposed to be very poor but for some reason they live in a house that is upper middle-class, a sitcom about identical cousins, a people from outer space sitcom, a teen angst sitcom, a sitcom featuring the jokes of some standup comedian starring that standup comedian, an elderly women sitcom, a sitcom with eight-year-old ninjas, a sitcom with a fat person, a sitcom that was perhaps once a comedy but is now a very serious drama that is not funny nor dramatic, a high school surf band sitcom, an important hospital sitcom, a sitcom with social commentary and adorable children, a people at work who don't seem to ever do any work sitcom, and a bunch of other sitcoms which seem to have no point but to exploit minorities.

Then the horror face hits the power button on his remote and the sitcom face collapses, his screen becomes black with a white dot that slowly fades away.

The horror face twirls his remote and slaps it into the holster on his thigh. Then goes back into the bar.

Sharp goes to the television head and kicks him.

"Dead," she says.

Oxy rubs his sideburns. "What the hell kind of shootout was that?"

Other television heads are running down the street at them. One of them has a sheriff's badge.

"Let's get out of here," Nixx says.

CHAPTER THREE

They dart into the saloon before the television-headed sheriff with a very loud monster truck show on his face can spot them.

Inside:

Dozens of wobbling people with television heads. Gunslingers playing poker and drunks and bartenders and scantily dressed women. They are very human from the shoulders down. They wear similar clothes to humans and move with similar body motions. The saloon girls have bodies just like the girls from Jackson, the same silky laced clothes with fluffy parts and high-heeled shoes, flirting with the gunslingers that are winning at poker.

The silent vampire movie faced Telosian is now comfortable at the head of one of the poker tables and is getting surrounded by several harlots with sexy detective shows on their screens, raccoon antennas like bows in their hair, caressing their human limbs around his back.

Random keeps behind Nixx and Oxy as they step up to the bar. Two television heads are drinking whiskey by dumping shots down slits like speaker holes on the sides of their heads.

The Telosians follow them with chaotic-flutter programs, trying to aim their screens in front of their faces. Death pushes away anyone who gets too close. Soon, all the people in the room are swarming them, sticking their electric heads into their path.

"Get back," Nixx squeals, pushing a short television head to the ground. "Do not invade this space," he says, outlining an invisible twenty-four inch border around his body. Oxy giggles with pleasure as the crowd tightens around them. Dozens of television shows swirling in their eyes, blinding them. Random goes dizzy when one of the electric harlots presses her screen against his face like a kiss. He sees her cat cartoon as tiny pixels of bright color and closes his eyes tight. Nixx has to pull him away from her willow-grip.

"Let's get out of here," Nixx says.

They pile out through a side door and cross the street. The strange people don't seem interested in them enough to leave the bar.

"What was that all about?" Random asks.

"Keep walking," Nixx says, his face at a 56 degree angle, concentrating on his footstep rhythm.

Death leads them into an inn that is of similar design to the saloon, probably owned by the same people, and goes upstairs to bed.

The others are left to deal with the innkeeper who buzzes at them with some old war movie on her face.

"How are we supposed to pay?" Sharp asks.

"Ignore her," Cry says. "Let's just find some empty rooms and go to sleep."

But before they make it halfway up the stairs, the innkeeper is outside buzzing through the streets with gun shots and cannon fires on her face. Getting the attentions of the TV-sheriff and his posse away from the dead sitcom face outside the saloon.

CHAPTER FOUR

The television heads stand in the doorway at Random and Sex, the others already upstairs in their rooms, slipping off their dirty clothes.

"What do we do?" Random asks.

"See what happens," Sex says.

The sheriff's monster truck show is blaring at them, his antennas sticking out of holes in his cowboy hat. The deputized TVs mock the sheriff in style. But they have several different program faces, from a baseball game to the weather channel to sitcoms to commercials with a totally-extreme-sports theme.

"They've got nice bodies," Sex says.

She approaches the sheriff and looks him up and down. "Terrible heads, but they're in shape," goes around to the back of them, "tight asses," and back to the front of the sheriff's screen. "Not bad."

She walks back to Random.

"Definitely worth a fuck," she says.

The television heads continue to stare at them. Heads blue-dazzling. The sheriff points at the furry gun in Random's pants.

"They want your gun," Cry says.

The sheriff draws his remote control and points it at

the young man.

"Should I give it to them?" Random asks.

Cry says, "No."

"I'm going to hand it over," Random says, hesitating in front of the strange gadget pointing at him, wondering if his face will mutate into something else if the sheriff pulls the trigger.

"Don't," Cry says.

Random pulls out his gun and the television heads leap back, whipping out their remote controls and clacking the buttons at the boy.

Nothing happens.

The crew keeps hitting the buttons at Sex and Random, but their weapons have no effect on them.

Cry shows her teeth to Random and begins to caress her backside. The remote controls continue to fire click-click-click-click-click. She coos at them, shaking her stegosaurus spikes.

Then Cry slides her blade from her back and lowers it into the sheriff's head.

The screen explodes into sparks and he crumbles to the ground. The others back away, still clicking their remotes at her. She swings her blade in a circle and smiles. The posse dissipates, running away while balancing their enormous heads.

"Look," Random says, pointing at the dead sheriff.

The smoke is clearing from the broken television. Underneath the screen there is a human-like face. A bloody skull in the box, covered in gluey liquid. It is still alive, gasping at the air, skinless, eyeballs popping out at them. Several wires grow from its skull into the television set, like metal nerves.

"Sexy," Cry says, smoothing her fingers across the bloody skull as it becomes limp.

She takes the sheriff's handcuffs and remote control, plucks the badge from his shirt and attaches it to a hook on her chest.

"What do you think?" Cry asks.

Random blinks at her.

She arches out her stegosaurus spikes and poses with the remote.

"There's a new lawman in town," she says in a fake cowboy accent.

Then she makes a gun with her fingers and winks at him.

CHAPTER FIVE

Upstairs:

Sharp and Oxy are tying a television woman to a chair.

"What are you doing?" Random asks.

"We want to watch her face," Oxy says.

The television woman squirms in her seat as they wrap her wrists and legs in rope. She's not one of the saloon girls from across the street. Her blue dress is not flashy enough to be a saloon girl. A morning talk show on her face.

There is something about her that reminds Random of Typi's older sister, Merth. A gorgeously bashful woman who would do anything to make you happy. Movements like a fawn, only making soft flowery sounds.

Oxy ties her neck and shoulders tight to the chair so that she can't move her head very well. And they pick her up off the ground and bring her into one of the rooms.

"Is there anymore of those up here?" Cry asks Nixx in the doorway.

Nixx points to a door at the end of the hall.

When Cry opens it, she sees one of them lying in a bed, fast asleep. His face is white with a high-pitched humming. A long black chord runs from the back of his head to an outlet on the wall.

She unplugs him and the television screen goes from

white to a horse racing show. He kicks his legs around when
Cry flips him onto his back and cuffs him.

"You're under arrest," she whispers into his ear/
speaker excitedly.

She pulls on his chord to wrench his head back,
stretching his spine into a curl. Then she ties the chord to his
ankles.

"This bed is your prison cell," she says.

Random is watching from the door. Cry glares at him.
She steps off the bed and creeps up into his face.

"You want me to arrest you too?" She rolls her enormous tongue at him.

Random blinks.

She sniffs at the sweat on his neck.

Then closes the door in his face.

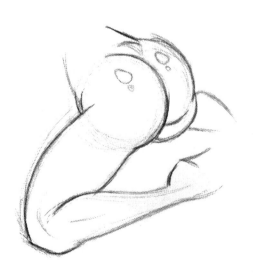

CHAPTER SIX

Nixx saunters into the room where Oxy and Sharp are piled on a fluffy bed, their eyes glued to the television woman's face. The greenish man looks out of the window. Television people are running around in circles in front of the inn. "What are we going to do about them?" Nixx asks the hermaphrodites.

They don't acknowledge him. They're on the edge of their seats.

"They look ready to tear this place down," Nixx says.

The others are hypnotized by the Telosian woman's eyes, like she's a radiant snake goddess.

Nixx sits down next to them.

The screen is playing a wrestling show. There are two enormous men wrestling two enormous men. One group of men dresses in flashy disco clothing with long hair and yellow beards. The other is a group of tough bikers with leather jackets and tattoos.

"What's this?" Nixx asks.

It takes a few minutes before he gets a response.

"I have no idea," Oxy says, "but it is the greatest thing I have ever seen in my life."

"There were people talking about a book before," Sharp

says. "We hit a knob on her cheek by accident and her face became this."

"What is this?" Nixx asks. "What are those guys doing?"

"Fighting!" Oxy cries. "Don't you know fightin' when you see it?"

Nixx looks at the motley wrestlers. One of them jumps off of a rope and catches another man's head between his thighs and pile-drives him into the mat.

"Oh!" Oxy cries. "They are such magnificent fighters! Look at them! So beautiful! Have you ever seen a man do anything like that before?"

A biker wrestler has a disco wrestler tied up in a knot.

"There's no way he can take that for much longer!" Oxy cries.

Nixx gets up and examines the young television woman, her body quivering under the ropes.

He sees two knobs on her face like Sharp said. Like tiny doorknobs. He turns one of them and the television woman twitches, her face changes from the wrestling show to a bunch of kids hopping up and down with plushy man-like animals.

"Bring them back!" Oxy screams.

Nixx returns her face to the wrestling show.

"I can't hear what she's saying about the fighters," Oxy says.

He waves his fist at the woman. "Speak up!"

Nixx tries turning the other knob and the television's voice grows louder. He turns it up until the dials are parallel.

"Ahhhh," Oxy says. "She has voice controls."

The voice says: And here comes the Iron Raider from behind! What's he got in has hand? Oh no, an aluminum baseball bat! You gotta be kidding me! Ooooooohhh, right in the spinal column of Bodacious Bobby! This is not looking good for the Disco Studs. Bodacious Bobby is on the ground, he's not moving, and Johnny Excitement can't reach him to make the tag. What are they going to do? Oh no, the Hell's Rollers get into the ring . . .

"Come on, Johnny Excitement!" Oxy screams.

Nixx shakes his head and shuffles out of the room to Random standing in the hallway.

"What's going on?" Nixx asks.

Random points down the stairs.

Through the open door, beyond the sheriff's corpse, a Telosian mob is forming. Very loud television programs jumble together into a screechy blur.

"She killed the sheriff?" Nixx asks.

Random nods.

"Why didn't she tell me?" Nixx smacks his thigh.

The television people storm into the entrance room until there is a flood of motion picture screens.

"We better move," Nixx says.

Random is already locking himself into one of the rooms.

CHAPTER SEVEN

Jesus Christ is dreaming about a flower with a skull in it. There aren't any people with arms or legs anywhere, just some torsos and a field of blue flowers where one flower grows petals from a little skull.

"This is the machine," a ratty voice says to him from behind.

But Jesus wakes before he turns around to the ratty voice and hears cluttering footsteps in the hallway.

He stands. Naked and dusty. Hair full of twigs and leaves. A musty scent in his crotch and underarms. His pubic hair is long and dreadlocked, burying his uncircumcised penis in knotty shrubs.

He takes a pistol from a holster on a chair and uses it to push open his door.

The hallway is full of television heads. They are just leaving, piling down the stairs. Death can hear the screams of Sharp as they drag her away.

Out the window: the television heads have Random, Nixx, and Oxy tied to nooses in the center of the street. They stand on chairs and have styrofoam looks on their faces.

Oxy snickers to himself.

Jesus puts his hat on and takes another pistol, then steps into the hallway.

The Telosians have already cleared out, and he strolls languidly scratching his bare ass with the barrel of a gun. He can hear Cry moaning behind one of the closed doors. Farther down, there are splinters of a door and Jesus can see the television woman still tied to a chair in an empty room, the wrestling program is on a commercial break and advertising some kind of canned Italian food for kids.

Death sees the television commercial and it kind of makes him hungry. He watches it for a while. Then the commercial goes back to wrestling and there is some very old wrestler with platinum blond hair and his wrestler girlfriend pointing and screaming about some things.

The television woman seems to lure Jesus closer with her flashy face. He steps into the room and sits down on the bed, very interested in what the wrestlers have to say.

Then the wrestler gets hit over the head with a chair and he collapses to the floor.

The audience is roaring and the wrestler's girlfriend screams.

Death regurgitates an oafish chuckle under his breath.

CHAPTER EIGHT

Nixx is very irritated because the four of them are not lined up evenly. Oxy's noose is twenty-eight inches away from Random's, and Random's is twenty-five inches away from his, and Sharp's, well Nixx can hardly stomach calculating the distance but it is at least forty-three inches away from his.

"It is utterly disgusting," Nixx mutters to himself.

Random is the only one praying. He is actually very annoyed that the others aren't praying with him. Who the hell do they think they are anyway, not praying to God with him? He wonders if they are not Christians, but then dismisses that thought immediately. *Everyone* is Christian, he says to himself. People have told him that there's such a thing as non-Christians but he doesn't believe them.

He nods his head and thinks, surely they must be praying to themselves . . .

The television people are surrounding them with their obnoxious programs. They just stand there, watching them, dizzying light across their faces.

On the next commercial break, Death comes outside with his pistols. Walking half-dazed with the wind chilling his naked skin.

The leader of the lynch mob turns to Death and before he can change his channel a bullet is put into his face. The other television heads freeze at the sight of their fallen leader. They peer through the smoking hole in his screen that continues as a hole in the man's inner goo-skull and brain.

Death yawns and scratches at himself.

A smaller Telosian, probably the son of the mob leader, screams a dirt bike racing show at Death and charges with his bare fists raised.

Without a flinch, Jesus fires and chunks of skull explode from the back of the boy's television head.

The Telosians disperse, running back into their buildings and locking their doors.

Death doesn't untie his friends right away. He goes back upstairs and finishes watching television first.

After he cuts them down, he says, "Get some sleep. The goblins will be here shortly after sundown."

Oxy giggles at his naked crinkled butt when he walks away from them.

CHAPTER NINE

They hope to get some sleep but right now they are too busy watching television. Oxy, Random, Death, and Sharp all piled together on the bed watching the TV woman who has given up struggling and sits slumped in her chair.

Nixx is the only one who doesn't really like to watch. He lies on the floor of the room and counts the hairs on his left arm. Last year he tried doing this but lost count after 245. This time he plans to finish or die trying. And then he will count the hairs on his right arm just to be sure they are even. He will become enraged if the arm hairs are not equal, because arm hairs are natural and he has come to rely on the geometrical correctness of things that are natural.

Normally Nixx wouldn't be counting his arm hairs in a room full of people who are most likely going to distract him, but he is nervous that the sun will go down while he isn't paying attention and will have to battle the black creatures all by himself. Not to mention Cry said she saw him die while she was masturbating and he's not yet sure if that was a joke or not, so that's got him high-strung. It will be a while before he'll want to be alone.

Cry walks into the room naked, dripping with hot wet.

"I'm taking a bath," she says to Nixx, even her stego-saurus-spikes dripping, hot metal, her pubic hairs smoothed to the contours of her crotch.

Nixx doesn't look at her, using his fingernails to separate the counted arm hairs from the uncounted arm hairs.

"You should take a bath too," Cry's face stern.

Nixx is trying not to look at her, even though he can sense her wet flesh above him, fighting the urge to look up at her. She bends down to him. "Do I have to carry you?" That's it. Her face is in front of his face. His counting ceases. His eyes crawling down her glistening snakeskin neck and shoulders, to shiny breasts draping down over his nose. Drops of hot bath drip from the nipples and slide down his cheek.

"I don't want to die," Nixx says underneath her.

Cry puts a spicy finger to his lips.

"Clean yourself," Cry says. "We need to fuck before you get killed tonight."

Then she pulls him to his feet and leads him by his pants into the bathroom.

Three tubs: two are filled with steaming water and one has a handcuffed television man inside.

She points at the television man. "That tub's his." She points at an empty tub. "This one's mine," and slides into the burning liquid.

Nixx rips his clothes trying to get out of them while Cry pulls at him, trying to get him inside the tub with or without his clothes. She pulls him ass-first into her lap, wrapping her legs around him. His boots still on, sticking out of the tub and attached to his pants and tan suspenders. He leaves them that way while Cry slithers her limbs around him, her spikes sticking out of the water and scraping the back of the tub.

"This is the machine," Cry says, stuffing Nixx's hand

into her cunt.

CHAPTER TEN

The sun goes down and the Telosians are outside carrying lanterns into a huge pile in the road.

"We should have made friends with them," Random says. "They could have helped us against the demons."

"They don't have any real guns," Sharp says. "They're deader than we are."

Death is wandering through the town, through stores and houses, trying to find more bullets for his gun. His fists squeeze frustrated as he pushes television people out of the way to look in their cabinets and trunks. He doesn't understand how they can have a civilization completely free of guns. He's seen the remotes, but doesn't understand how they can be considered weapons. You don't load them. You don't shoot anything out of them. You can't practice with beer bottles. You can't look dangerous holding one. And they can't kill anything but television shows.

"What good are they?" Jesus says to a Telosian family.

They play soap operas at him.

Oxy is still in the same spot on the bed, glued to the television set.

Cry, naked and dripping dry in front of him, says,

"What's so interesting about her?"

Oxy points at her television head. A science-fiction show is on about some people on a spaceship.

Cry sits next to Oxy and leans forward, trying to get interested in the show he is watching.

The show is now talking about some aliens who are absurdly logical and have long ears like Nixx.

Oxy has no idea what is going on but he loves it anyway. He wants Cry to love it too but she doesn't seem to be enjoying herself. She can't sit still. She shifts forward and back. Looks around the room and at a daisy-painting in the hall. She squeezes her palm into the flab of her thigh and bites a tattooey finger.

"I'll make it better," she says.

Pulling the blade from a pocket of her flesh, Cry steps to the television woman and cuts her shirt open, exposing human breasts that are not very large but have curvy long nipples. Piece by piece, she cuts the dress out from under the ropes. The television woman squirms wildly now and Cry gets an electric shock when she slips the woman's nipple between her lips.

She pinches a thanks to the nipple and sits back down, admiring the naked body with the television head.

"That's better," she says to Oxy.

But Oxy loves the face so much he doesn't care about the figure. He was beginning to forget there was even a person attached to the television set.

Cry exits the room and goes back to Nixx wiping off the smeared green paint from his face. She can sense his wormy nerves.

"What are they anyway?" he asks.

"Goblins," Cry says. "That's what Death calls them."

"Goblins?"

"But they are just humans that have become wrong," she says. "You saw what happened to the hermaphrodite on the train."

"He was turning black."

"He was infected with their disease. It is a plague that makes people demon-like."

"Goblin plague?"

"Like the black death, leprosy."

"Where did it come from?" Nixx asks.

"A dark spidery place."

"Have you seen this in your sex?"

Cry nods. "Years ago. I was fucking both Jesus and Battle Johnny at the time. They saw it too."

"That's why they came to Jackson, to warn everybody?"

"But the townspeople thought they were under attack," Cry responds. "They started killing the hermaphrodites."

"And then the black creatures came," Nixx says.

"They shouldn't have tried to save Jackson. They should've known nobody would believe them."

"I believed them. If they didn't come I would've been killed."

"You'll be killed anyway," Cry says.

"Tonight, you say?" Nixx asks.

"Tonight," Cry says.

Nixx repaints his face. But this time, instead of solid green, he paints his skull on the outside of his skin.

Then, a little while later: "Can the Telosians get infected by the disease?"

Cry says, "I don't know. My vision said that no Telosian would fall victim to the disease, so I think maybe they are immune. In any case, Telos is the safest place for us to be."

"Not safe for me," Nixx says.

"No," Cry says. "No place is safe for you."

"Should I try to fight fate?"

"If you want to."

They make love again in one of the bedrooms and collapse on their sides facing each other. They are lazy-drugged from sex. Nixx sees the future again, but the future has nothing to do with him. It shows a landscape full of babies. Something like a painting.

"I think I'll create a work of art," Nixx says.

"Art?"

"I always wanted to create something." He closes his eyes. "I always planned on doing something significant."

"You don't have time for art," Cry says. "The goblins will be here soon."

"Perhaps I die because I am creating art rather than fighting to survive."

"Perhaps."

"Fate can be an ugly thing . . ."

"Shut up," Cry says. "Let's fuck again."

"I am like a slave to fate."

"You're like a slave to my cunt," Cry says, angry face looking down on him.

CHAPTER ELEVEN

The goblins aren't here yet and it's been dark for a few hours. Oxy has just been watching television and he only moves when he has to take a leak out the window, still looking over his shoulder so he doesn't miss anything.

He curls his sideburns and licks a tooth.

"There's no place on Earth you'd rather be than Hampshire Mall," says the television.

Oxy wishes he could go to that mall.

Random and Sharp are sticking close to Death, following him around the room as he washes his underwear and draws little pictures of teddy bears on the wall with nail rust.

"This is where everyone dies," Death tells them.

They nod their heads.

"There's just not enough bullets."

Outside, the Telosians have constructed a circus tent. The whole town must be there, a couple hundred of them crowding into the tent and mixing their television shows together.

"What are they up to?" Nixx says to Cry looking out of a window.

"Having a circus," she says.

The Telosians are just sitting in there, staring at each other and coated in flickery lantern light.

"They picked the wrong night for that," Nixx says.

Sharp is sitting in a chair, playing with raggy television dolls.

After a few more hours of waiting, Cry slams reptilian knuckles on a deck of cards and takes Nixx across the street to have a drink at the tavern.

"This is driving me nuts," Cry says. "I wish those things would just attack and get it over with."

Nixx shrugs.

The tavern is empty but the door is unlocked and all the lights are still lit. Cry swipes a bottle of whiskey from behind the bar and nicks the green-skulled man's cheek with her spiky backside, just flirting with him. She pours him a glass while the blood trickles and Nixx's face is blank.

"You don't act like a Hoak," Cry tells him.

He sips his whiskey.

"You look Hoak," Cry says. "You've got Hoak ears, the Hoak face paint, Hoak arrows."

Nixx coughs at the liquor fumes.

Cry drinks from the bottle, black lips enveloping most of the neck. "You are hard to figure out. You act nice and neat like an Easterner. Yet you dress like you're a rough gunman, like one of Battle Johnny's men. And you're a Hoak."

"I don't like to talk about it," Nixx says.

Cry jiggles her spikes and drinks some more. The lights flicker orange against the curve of her jaw. Then taunts, "Was your mommy raped by an Indian?"

"I said—" Nixx threatens with a hand on his holster.

Cry cackles at him. She continues until Nixx lowers his eyes and relaxes his hand.

He says, "It's no big deal, anyway."

"Sure it is," Cry says. "Your Eastern mother was raped by a savage Hoak, maybe several savage Hoaks."

Nixx frowns.

She continues, "Then maybe you grew up in a rough western town. Being part Hoak, you probably had to learn to fight at an early age. Your mother probably married a man who beat you day and night."

The green-faced man kicks the seat out from under him and paces the bar. He takes a new bottle of whiskey and chokes down a shot.

"It was nothing like that," he says.

Cry smiles. "Then tell me."

He takes another drink and wheezes. This whiskey must have come from a different batch that was poorly distilled.

Cry pulls him back to his seat. "I'm going to assume I'm right unless you tell me."

Nixx gets comfortable and starts to feel a bit dizzy. He is beginning to get drunk. Maybe too drunk. He wonders if the whiskey is what gets him killed tonight.

"I shouldn't be drinking," Nixx says. "It's your fault."

"My fault?"

"You're wrong about me. And you're wrong about Hoaks."

"You can't be full Indian. You're too pale."

"Hoaks aren't savage. They're peaceful. And they're smarter than whites. Even more technologically advanced."

"Advanced? Indians? Ha!" Cry pounds her fist on the table.

"You people don't understand. You think all the tribes are exactly the same. All weak ignorant primitives. But every tribe is unique in their own ways. Many are superior to you."

"Now you're just being funny."

"Some tribes are spiritually superior, some are poetically superior, some are physically superior. Hoaks are technically superior."

"That's enough."

"It's true."

"But what about your mixed genes?"

"My what?"

"Your race," Cry says. "You're a half-breed. Somebody had to be raped to make you. Either your father or your mother was white and one of them raped the other."

"No one was raped," Nixx says, "and most Hoaks are half-breeds."

"They must get raped a lot."

"No one gets raped!" Nixx squeezes the dizziness behind his eyes. "It is our culture."

"What does that mean?"

"It's just our culture. Leave me alone."

Nixx stands up and hurries out of the tavern.

CHAPTER TWELVE

Cry follows the Hoak boy, waving two whiskey bottles at him and blowing kisses with puffy black lips.

He darts into the circus tent and the woman chugs liquor as she stumbles in after him.

Inside:

The television people are all sitting in a giant circle, motionless. Very loud television shows pointed at a totem pole in the center of the ring. The leader of the chant is a muscular man in a priest's cassock, his screen larger than any other in Telos. He watches Cry carefully as she creeps around their meditation.

Cry doesn't see Nixx. She walks around the outside of the Telosian circle, trying to block out the scratchy TV noises.

The pole in the center of the ring is not exactly a totem pole. It is a spiraling sculpture made of sewn together cockroaches and birds and half a bull. Twisting and shuffling.

Cry sees an open flap on the far side of the tent and guesses Nixx weaseled away. Her spirit becomes clicker-waves with alcohol as she goes after him.

The spinning totem pole begins to whistle and spray a squidy juice at the television sets. Arms and screens stretch to receive this thick liquid. Then they take off all of their clothes.

The spiky woman sees all of the nudity, but decides not to indulge herself. The fishy smells are too strong for her.

Before she leaves the tent, she finds Nixx crouching in a dark corner. He leaps up and grabs her by the waist. Twists her into circles and sucks in her spicy lips.

They continue spinning in a circle as they kiss, like a mirror image of the fleshy rotating totem pole that spits whiskey saliva instead of squid juice.

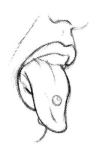

CHAPTER THIRTEEN

Bleary-eyed Random is lying in a dry tub. He has a straight razor and is wondering if he shouldn't slit his own throat with it. A square ladybug crawls across his chin.

There's an unconscious Telosian in another tub.

"We need to stick with the others," Sharp says from the doorway.

Random nods and puts the razor away.

"Those things should be here any second." Sharp cleans her nails with a fork. "I can feel them all around us."

Random has an ear in one hand. His lower lip sags gently at the hermaphrodite.

"I'm still a virgin," he says.

Sharp cleans her spectacles.

"I got married yesterday and my wife died before we could even consummate the marriage." He scratches at a drop of blood on his sleeve and frowns.

Sharp nods her head and goes up to the attic, an empty place of white powders and webs. Death is here, digging through an old chest in search of bullets.

On a shelf, there are jars filled with seasons. There is a jar of tiny winter, jars of tiny springs, autumns, and dozens of jars of summers. She wonders if the season will change if she opens a jar. She wonders what will happen if she drinks a season or rubs it on her belly.

Beneath the seasons she finds transparent paper-thin clothes labeled: Music, forest, and lunch.

Wide eyes, like she found just what she's always been looking for. She wads the glassy suits into a little ball and hides them under her shirt.

Death doesn't seem to notice her. He is playing with a toy truck and cursing himself.

CHAPTER FOURTEEN

Sharp goes into an empty room and examines the strange suits. They have a stretchy latex feeling to them. She removes her clothes, exposing shriveled hairy breasts and a penis/vagina combination. And pulls on the suit marked "Forest". The suit is tight-forming, like a second layer of skin.

Once on, it changes. Deep green colors swirl across her flesh, until her body becomes a painting of a forest. No, a moving painting. The trees are swaying in the wind and she can see tiny birds inside of her.

Like a Telosian's face, she thinks.

Her new forest body looks sexy to her. Much better than her regular body. She goes to rub her curves, but her hands slip inside of the forest. She can feel the trees and the crisp air. There are birds chirping and deer sharpening their antlers.

She looks at herself in a mirror. The light of the forest brightens the room. She smiles and cries and laughs to herself.

The mirror shatters. Sharp looks on the ground of broken glass to find a bloody twitching dove that had flown out of her chest.

She picks it up, pets the blood out of its feathers, and drops it inside of her torso.

Then goes back to smiling/crying/laughing . . .

CHAPTER FIFTEEN

Random is out in the desert, sickle-running, aimlessly. Something is after him. Screeching baby-cries all around him in the darkness. Gurgles, white-bubble movements.

He doesn't know how he got outside or where he's going. But he's running away from Telos, deeper into the unknown wilds. The lights from the town disappear from view. Stumbling. He doesn't look back.

Blind and nerve-flooded, his heart punching out of his throat and eyeballs.

He runs until his body goes limp. His face collapses into the hard dirt and blood pops out of his nose.

CHAPTER SIXTEEN

Morning comes. Nixx and Cry wake in a worm-mud puddle in the middle of the road, with gila-scorpions clipping at their knuckles.

"Don't move, they're poisonous," Cry says.

"I'm not moving," Nixx replies.

Nixx isn't moving.

"They lock into your skin with their jaws and sting you repeatedly with their tails. You have to cut off their heads to get them to stop."

"You don't know anything about gila-scorpions," Nixx says.

Cry frowns at him.

The gila-scorpions are squatting up and down at them.

"I didn't die during the night," Nixx says. "The creatures never came."

"So?" Cry draws her blade and cuts the insect-lizards into halves.

"You told me I'd die in the night."

Cry shrugs.

"You lied to me."

"I didn't lie," she says. She stands and wipes mud from her legs. "I was just off by a day. You'll surely die tonight."

"I didn't see my death when we made love last night. I

saw pianos."

"You don't always see what you're looking for," Cry says.

Cry stretches in the soft morning sun. It's quiet. Not even birds chirping. The Telosian circus tent is down and wadded against the side of the road. Dead campfires expel willowy strings of smoke.

"What do you think they were doing last night?" Cry asks.

"Some kind of religious ceremony," Nixx says. "Most likely."

"It really got me going after that juice sprayed on us."

"It was probably some kind of drug," Nixx says, slow blinking eyes.

Cry bites her lip.

"I think I'm going to like these people," Cry says. "There's something inside of me," she rubs the skin below her belly button, "that's telling me these people have a lot of potential. I think there's a real future for me in this town."

Nixx is trying to reassemble the gila-scorpions, placing their bodies in a perfectly straight line exactly two inches apart. Cry stands over him and presses her bare feet against his hands.

"Too bad you won't be around to help me," she says.

"You never know," Nixx says. "You were wrong about last night. I might not die for a long time."

Cry smirks and shakes her head at him.

CHAPTER SEVENTEEN

Nixx and Cry walk in on Death sticking his hands in and out of Sharp's torso.

"What are you doing?" Cry asks.

It is raining inside of Sharp's forest skin. Jesus is washing his hands in the water.

"I found it in the attic," Sharp says.

Cry's eyes light up. She sticks her face through Sharp's back and wets her hair, drinks the raindrops. "I want one!"

"I've got three," Sharp says. "They are all different."

"Go put another one on," Cry says.

Sharp comes back with another skin. This one puts a city inside of her. Mile-high skyscrapers, thousands of honking cars, smog pouring into the room.

"Take it off! Take it off!" the others say.

Sharp leaves and returns with food inside of her skin.

"Yummy!" Cry says. She pulls a cupcake out of her butt cheek and takes a bite. "It's sweet!"

Jesus pulls hamburgers out of her belly and Nixx pulls a ten foot chain of linked sausages from her crotch.

"Don't eat too much of her," Cry says. "She'll die."

Sharp shakes her head. She empties all of the food out of her arm onto the table. Then removes her arm from the sleeve. It is perfectly fine. Her flesh has not been turned to food like Cry suspected. When Sharp inserts her arm back into the skin, all the food has been replenished.

"Where's Random and Oxy?" Nixx asks.

"Oxy is upstairs," Sharp says. "I haven't seen the kid."

Nixx searches upstairs and finds only Oxy asleep in front of the television girl, missing a show with burly muscled women wearing American flags for underwear. Random is nowhere to be seen.

Nixx walking downstairs, "We should look for him."

The others sag with disinterested faces.

"He's probably dead," Jesus says. "He wasn't very strong. Anything could've killed him."

They search the town but only find Telosians with their heads plugged into walls, high-pitched hums for faces.

Above the saloon, caged animal smells, there's a group of gnarly black-clothed Telosians lined against the walls facing each other. Also with blank-hum screens.

Cry claws at a man's bare chest, cat-growling at him and licks flakes of skin from her fingernails.

"What are you doing?" Sharp hisses.

The Telosian wakes and his face turns into an angry b&w horror movie with a golem walking through a village.

Cry snickers when the man reaches for his remote control.

He draws it and his hand falls off as he points it at her face, not realizing the blade she was holding in front of him. The television channel changes to thousands of screaming Japanese people running through the streets of Tokyo to escape Rodan.

Blood rivers out of the Telosian's wrist as he flails out of his seat, rolling across the splintery floor and knocking the other men out of their seats.

The rest of them wake up with more angry horror shows. They shoot at Cry with their remotes, but nothing happens. They don't understand why.

Outside:

Jesus has found Random in a terrible state. His face is bloody. His tongue is dry and swollen. He can hardly speak.

"What happened?" Cry asks, as she steps out of the saloon, lick-cleaning her blade.

"The desert . . ." Random says. "It's alive."

"Show us," Death says.

CHAPTER EIGHTEEN

They leave town to the west and discover the landscape has changed. It is not desert anymore. It's just . . . babies. Millions of them. Human babies growing from plants. They are all that can be seen for miles. Screaming, sleeping, wiggling, cooing, gurgling, pooping, crying babies.

"I always wanted a baby!" Sharp says.

She dances into the babies like a field of sunflowers.

"Were these here before?" Cry asks.

"I was being chased by the creatures last night," Random chokes. "I was knocked unconscious last night and about an hour ago I woke up in a pile of babies. I had to step carefully through them to get back to town."

Sharp plucks her favorite baby from the field, a plump blue-eyed girl, and brings her back to the others.

"Are you going to keep that?" Nixx asks.

"I can't have children of my own," she says, kitty-eyes glazed over at the child jiggling in her arms.

CHAPTER NINETEEN

Back in town:

The gang of black-clothed remote-slingers with horror movie faces has gathered in the middle of town, waiting for the outsiders. Their leader is in the front with a long trench coat spinning in the breeze, Nosferatu on his face. And in his hand: a gun. A *real* gun. Not a remote control. It is extremely old and rust-candied, but will work. The Telosian waves it over his head at his opponents, surprising them with the new weapon. He glances at his brother next to him, the one with blood gushing out of his wrist in cartoonishly large splashes.

He wants justice.

Jesus nods at him and steps forward. The Nosferatu Telosian holsters his rust-pistol and nods his enormous head back at Jesus.

Facing each other, hands out to their sides, Jesus throwing the right side of his trench coat behind his thigh to reveal a black widow pistol.

Jesus allows his opponent to go for his gun first. The Telosian draws and both guns fire at the same time. But Jesus' bullet hits first, right in the screen. Exploding the television head, and Sharp's baby cheers at the cloud of smoke.

There is a bullet hole in Jesus' hair below his left ear.

His hair is so matted that Sharp can see a perfectly round hole. She closes one eye and peers through it to see Nixx on the other side.

Nixx is on the ground with a bullet in his chest.

Cry kicks him.

No response.

"Dead," she says.

Sharp and Random back away.

Two of the Telosians, including the one with a missing hand, are fighting over the rusty gun. The pistol falls apart in their hands. Christ fires his gun two more times and makes two more clouds of smoke.

The rest of the raggedy Telosian gang doesn't move. They stare at Jesus with ghostly TV shows on mute. They make sudden movements that force the grim reaper to go for his other pistol, but the movements aren't aggressive. Jesus relaxes his arm, confused face, when he realizes they are applauding him, cheering with golden-age Hollywood movies.

Even though he killed their leaders.

CHAPTER TWENTY

The Telosian gang makes Jesus Christ their leader/savior/god. He is invincible and will make them invincible.

Almost dusk, in the saloon: Jesus is party-king with the Telosians. He is at the table chugging bottles of whiskey with chubby television whores on his thighs.

Sharp at another table with Random, crouching her shoulders to shield her baby from the splashing whiskey and blaring television shows.

"It'll be night soon," Random tells her. "What are they doing?"

Sharp is captured by the infant's smile.

"They said they were going to barricade the town . . ." Random's voice is barely audible in the television ooze.

Cry descends the staircase. Two Telosian men and a woman behind her, straightening their clothes rubbing the sweat from their necks.

"What are we going to do?" Random asks Cry when she sits down next to him and lights a cigar.

"About the goblins?" Cry asks, blowing smoke out of her teeth.

Random nods. "It's getting dark."

"Not sure there's anything we can do," Cry says.

She goes to Jesus' table, sits across from him and steals one of his chubby whores.

"What do you think you're doing?" Cry asks.

"Making friends!" Christ is very animated. He is gargle-laughing and chattering everyone's ears off. The complete opposite of his usual calm/quiet/depressed demeanor. "I learned their language and can communicate with them now! They say they will help fight the goblins! We have nothing to worry about!"

"I don't care about the goblins," Cry says. "I just don't want you taking over this town. These people are special. I want them."

Jesus' face drops. His voice is no longer happy-toned when he says, "You can't have them."

"They're mine," she says. "Stay away from them."

"I'm willing to share them with you," he says with black/broken teeth. "But I won't give them up."

Cry says, "I've seen the future. They aren't for you. Keep away."

With that, Cry whips around, nicking Christ's knuckles with her stegosaurus spikes, and stomps out of the saloon with most of his television whores.

CHAPTER TWENTY-ONE

Sharp comes back from the bathroom into the saloon. It is late in the night, most of the Telosians are passed out or plugged into outlets upstairs. There is just one table awake, with Jesus and three Telosians playing poker. The bartender is back in the kitchen washing dishes.

She goes to the gambling table to reclaim her baby from Christ and jumps in shock when she sees the condition of her new child. It is covered from head to toe in yellow bruises, it's skin loose and droopy, very sickly. It's mouth is sagging open but it doesn't cry or gurgle.

"What did you do to her?" Sharp screams at Jesus.

The gunslinger is busy trying to keep his eyes from rolling back into his head, unable to concentrate on his cards or Sharp's words.

She slams her tiny fist onto the table in front of him and he wakes up. "How could you beat an infant?" she cries.

Jesus grunts when he sees the baby. "How did that happen?"

"You tell me. She was fine ten minutes ago."

Jesus shrugs and moves his eyes to the television shows.

Sharp begins to twitch her neck at him. She hasn't had that twitch since before she met Battle Johnny.

"Don't ignore me!" she screams, spitting on the deck of cards. She's scared to touch the baby, worried it's skin is too sensitive to be touched.

Jesus stops looking at the Telosians and turns to Sharp. "They say that it isn't a baby."

"What?" Sharp asks.

"It's not really a baby. It's a piece of fruit."

"What the hell are you talking about?" she asks.

Jesus holds up his hand like a stop sign at Sharp and a Telosian passes him a butcher knife.

"Look," he says, and chops the baby in half with the knife. The baby is in two pieces and still wiggling and gurgling like nothing happened. The infant's insides are not human. They are the like the insides of a watermelon. Juicy, red, with black and white seeds.

"See?" Jesus says. "Fruit."

He cuts a slice from the gurgling baby and takes a bite. Sharp's face is frozen at him, blank eyes, mouth agape. She can't say a word as the gunslinger devours her baby.

"Delicious," he says, licking his lips.

He gets up and takes the baby's upper half with him. He gets a spoon from the kitchen and shovels red balls out of its gut.

Sharp doesn't react until the baby is hollow of fruit and no longer moving. Just a baby-shaped rind pushed to the edge of the table.

Her reaction is: a high-pitched shriek that makes the glasses crackle.

She races out of the saloon, out of town, into the dark landscape to the west.

The fields are no longer filled with babies, but old men and women. They stand silent and crouched over in the moonlit desert.

Sharp picks up a stone and runs through the field smashing the elderly. They don't flinch or utter a word as they explode with juicy sweet redness. Sharp screams at them, pops their heads off, kicks their stomachs in.

In a blind rage that echoes in the night.

The Corruption of
Television Town

CHAPTER ONE

A glittery silver morning.

The demons did not attack last night.

Sharp awakes covered in sticky elderly fruit juice and sludge and fruit flies, in the middle of a field of pianos. The baby/people/fruit fields have rotted away and in their place are hundreds of grand pianos, evenly placed six feet apart from each other across the landscape, into the horizon.

Sharp doesn't remember falling asleep here. She must have exhausted herself and passed out on the spot. Just as Random did the night before.

Stepping through the maze of pianos, she hears one of them being played very poorly in the distance near the town. The song is disturbing to Sharp. The tune is being played in perfect rhythm, but it is lacking in composition. It is simplistic, emotionless, and ugly to the ears. Getting closer, she notices a man with his shirt off, in front of a piano. She figures it is Random, because it definitely cannot be Jesus or Oxy.

But, no, on closer inspection she discovers it is Nixx. He is not dead anymore, not wearing any green paint, and he wears only pants and a bandage for the bullet wound on his chest.

"I thought you were dead?" Sharp asks upon arrival.

Nixx stops piano-playing and shakes his head. "I woke up in a pool of blood, all alone."

Sharp notices his bandage has been wrapped very precisely around his torso and shoulder. He is extremely clean. Sterilized.

"What happened here?" she asks, looking at the pianos.

"The Telosians told Jesus that there is a different landscape for every day of the week. What day is it? Monday? I guess it's a piano landscape every Monday. A baby landscape every Sunday. God knows what there'll be tomorrow."

Nixx goes back to playing piano. He concentrates really hard to hit each key in perfect timing, placing a perfectly even amount of finger-weight on the keys every time, his fingers raising at just the right height between notes. But his mind is so occupied with his finger movements and calculations that he can't pay attention to the music. It just sounds mechanical, eerie.

"Have you played a piano before?" Sharp asks, snotty-voiced.

Nixx shakes his head, his tongue on the side of his mouth for concentration. "I don't have the time to learn how to play, but I need to create something right now. I'd rather create something horrible than die knowing I never created anything at all."

Sharp nods and leaves him alone. The piano music is unnerving and sleeping in the dirt has given her a headache.

CHAPTER TWO

Sharp meets Random near the edge of town. He is handcuffing a Telosian farmer's daughter.

"What are you doing?" Sharp asks.

He points at a badge on his chest. "I've been deputized."

"By who?"

"Cry," he spits and flexes minuscule muscles. "She's the sheriff now. She told me that all the young women in town have committed horrible crimes and must be arrested immediately."

"What crimes?"

"I don't know," he says. "She wouldn't tell me. I'm only the deputy."

Sharp follows Random and his young Telosian prisoner with a children's game show on her face.

"So which side are you going to be on?" Random asks her.

Sharp says, "What do you mean?"

"You didn't know? Jesus and Cry have cut the town in half. Cry has claimed the western side of town and Jesus took the east."

"What for?" Sharp asks.

"They each want to be boss of the town," he says. "But they don't want to share. They divided it in half and Nixx says it won't be too long before there's a war between the two factions. You should pick a side."

"What side are the others on?"

"I'm with Cry. Oxy is with Jesus. Stupid Nixx refuses to take sides. You should join Cry's team. She promises to have sex with everyone who joins her."

Random has a big goofy smile that he can't control.

"Don't have sex with her," Sharp says. "She's poison."

CHAPTER THREE

Random doesn't take his prisoner to jail, but to church.

There is a new sign out front:

EJACULATION CHURCH

"What is this?" Sharp asks.

"It's where the girls have to do their community service," Random says.

"It's a whore house!" Sharp cries as she sees the Telosian women in the doorway. "She turned the church into a damn whore house!"

"All buildings on this side of town have become whore houses," Random says. "The inn, the general store, the schoolhouse, the barbershop. She wants the town to revolve around sex."

"Where is she?" Sharp asks. "I want to talk to her."

Random drops off the scared television girl into the hands of older experienced prostitutes who wrap their arms around her, static sparks when they touch their screens together.

"She's busy right now," Random says. "But you can see her later."

"She's got a lot of explaining to do," Sharp says.

Random isn't listening to her. He has a bulge in his pants and can't take his eyes off of a particularly busty Telosian women's cleavage.

CHAPTER FOUR

Sharp goes to the inn, another whorehouse, and gets some sleep in an empty bedroom full of lingering sex-smells.

She wakes and returns to the ejaculation church.

It is like an orgy in the streets. There is sex scattered across the porches, dangling out of windows, piled on the side of the road. All of the regular townsfolk have been transformed into prostitutes and horny television-headed men with soft-core porn films for faces.

"She's not here," Random says, his voice calm and stern. He's recently lost his virginity to one of the television whores. "You'll have to come back another time."

Sharp waits for awhile, but Cry doesn't show up. She gets hungry and goes into Jesus' side of town, to the saloon. After an hour of waiting around, she realizes that she's not going to get any food. They don't even seem to have food here. None of the Telosians are eating. The kitchen is just a sink of water for washing glasses.

She watches Jesus in a rocking chair, drinking from a bottle of whiskey and shooting through the saloon window at the local townspeople walking by. There are a few corpses in the street, but most of his victims were only shot in the arms or legs.

He's using the furry gun that Battle Johnny had found. It shoots silently like arrows.

"Can you believe it?" waving his gun at the crowd. "I've been firing for hours and it's still not empty. Unlimited bullets!"

Their television shows flicker at him.

Nixx enters the saloon and sits next to Sharp.

"Can you believe them?" he asks her. "Splitting up the town like this . . ."

"They treat them like animals," Sharp says.

"Something's terribly wrong with those two," Nixx says.

They pause as a Telosian man vomits liquid television shows out of his screen. It is some kind of futuristic cop show, which continues on the sparkly pool of vomit by his feet.

"Have you found any food?" Sharps asks.

"No," Nixx says. "I've been too nervous to eat."

"There isn't any food anywhere," she says. "I don't think these people eat like we do."

"We'll have to eat out of your food-skins," he says.

Sharp makes a squinty face at Jesus. He is scratching his crotch with the furry gun.

She sighs. "If the creatures attack us tonight we're dead for sure."

"We might want to forget about the others," Nixx says. "We'll have to figure something out on our own."

CHAPTER FIVE

Nixx and Sharp searching for a safehouse:
"The jail and the bank are probably our best bets," Nixx says.

Sharp licks dust from her glasses. "But the other towns had banks and jailhouses yet nobody survived."

"They were also caught by surprise," Nixx says.

Cry is outside of the jailhouse, leaning against the door like she owns the place. She wears a crab on her head as a cowboy hat. The crab legs dangling down the side of her face like locks of hair.

"Come to be deputized?" she asks with a big black smile.

"No," Nixx says.

She frowns at him.

"We think those creatures might be back tonight," Sharp says.

"I told you," Cry says. "We're safe in Telos."

"How can you be sure?" Nixx asks.

"I have seen it in my cum," she says. "The black goblins never make it this far."

"We're going to play it safe," Nixx says.

"Can we reinforce one of the prison cells?" Sharp asks.

"So we can have a safe place to retreat just in case they come back?"

"I need the cells for prisoners," Cry says. "You're not allowed in them unless you want to become my prisoners?" Cry raises an eyebrow at them.

"Let's go," Nixx says, turning his back.

Sharp catches Cry sticking her long lizard tongue out at Nixx like a pissy four-year-old.

CHAPTER SIX

Random is fucking a Telosian whore again. The same one he lost his virginity to earlier in the day.

She is on top of him, holding his wrists down on the bed. Even though they don't know how to communicate with each other, she can tell he is very new to sex. And she seems to be turned on by his innocence.

Cry hand-picked this whore for Random. She must have known this one likes to corrupt the innocent.

Her face is playing a show called "The Greatest American Hero." There is a man in red pajamas flying very poorly through the air and crashing into buildings. But Random doesn't care about the show. He likes watching the woman's pointy breasts bobbing up and down as she pumps into him.

When she climaxes she jerks her body at him and slams his face into her glass screen. Random's nose bursts into a bloody mess. He feels warm fluid dribbling onto his lips.

The Telosian woman continues to fuck Random, very slowly, blood on her face. She leans closer to him, as if staring into his eyes. The television show goes to mute and changes to a soap commercial. His orgasm oozes out as a static tongue stretches out of her television and licks his blood off of her screen. She leans in and licks the blood from his lips, then sticks her television tongue into his mouth.

Random can feel the soap commercial inside of him. The woman on the screen is caressing her silky smooth leg as it slides down his throat.

CHAPTER SEVEN

Sharp and Nixx go to the bank. It is on Cry's side of town but has yet to be turned into a whorehouse. There are a few yellow-stained mattresses on the floor so surely they have plans for its future. Other than that the place is empty.

"This won't work," Sharp says. "The walls aren't thick enough."

"I'm hoping the vault will work," Nixx says.

"Some of these small town banks don't have vaults," Sharp says. "They probably just have a big safe."

Behind the counter there is a big black safe.

"See," Sharp says.

Nixx enters the backroom. A record office. There is a dead Telosian on the floor. His neck broken.

"It must be easy to break their necks with all that weight on their heads," Sharp says.

Nixx finds another door. "Over here."

Sharp rubs her hand across the Telosian's blank screen and static crackles between her fingers.

There is a vault beyond the door. It has been emptied recently. Probably by Jesus Christ and his gang of horror movie thugs.

"Will it work?" Sharp asks.

"It's better than nothing," Nixx says. "Let's fill this up

with supplies now so it'll be ready for tonight."

"I'll make some beds for us in here," Sharp says. "We can make it our home."

CHAPTER EIGHT

Oxy gets married to his Telosian woman in the saloon.

He doesn't wear a suit. He is shirtless and has a television painted on his belly with a wrestler flexing his muscles on the screen.

Jesus Christ is drunk enough to give the ceremony but most of his words are mumbled. The only words Oxy can somewhat make out are "I now pronounce you man and wife."

Oxy doesn't seem to care what the Telosian woman has to say about all this. He can't understand her anyway. She is still tied up and he doesn't have plans to untie her anytime soon.

His large hairy breasts bulge against hers as he kisses the bride's reality TV show.

CHAPTER NINE

By nightfall, after Nixx and Sharp are safely locked away in the town's vault, an enormous party forms.

There has been a bit of partying going on all day long, especially on Death's side of town, but now that the sun has gone down it is time to get serious.

Actually, there are two separate parties happening. One on Jesus Christ's side and one on Cry's side.

The party on Death's side is very violent. There are fights breaking out constantly. So many that you can't tell who is fighting who. It is like a bar room brawl has stretched out of the bar and enveloped the entire neighborhood.

Cry's side of town, the party looks very similar. But instead of fighting, everyone is having sex. It is like an orgy has stretched outside of the whorehouse and enveloped the entire neighborhood.

Random is a bit overwhelmed by it all and has to take a step back from all the fighting and fucking. He climbs a ladder and watches the chaos from on top of the jailhouse.

He can see the whole town from up there. He can see both Death and Sex on their opposite sides of town. The parties revolve around each of them like hurricanes. The closer the partiers are to the eye of Jesus' party, the more violent they become. In the outskirts of his party, people are just gently shoving each other and laughing. Near the core of his party, people are stabbing and shooting each other. And Death Himself obliterates anybody who gets within arms reach.

In the outskirts of Cry's party, everyone is kissing and flirting. But near the center, it is all hardcore extreme sex. Bondage, rape, shitting, double-anal. Sex Herself is surrounded by six guys and six girls, and is somehow able to pleasure all twelve of them with her body at the same time.

Random doesn't see Cry and Death as traveling companions anymore. He sees them as gods.

CHAPTER TEN

Nixx and Sharp can hear the party from inside the vault but aren't sure what is going on.

"They could be getting ripped apart by the demons for all we know," Nixx says.

Sharp nods and rests her head on his naked thigh.

"I've never had it like that before," she says, closing her eyes.

"Me . . . neither," Nixx says.

His eyebrows have been frozen in a high-stretched position for at least ten minutes.

"I mean, Battle Johnny was all man on the outside, but in his pants he was mostly woman. His penis . . . it never really worked. When we made love, it was my dick that would fuck his vagina. Nobody's ever fucked my vagina until now."

She rubs her cheek against his penis and says, "It was nice."

Nixx cringes.

He doesn't know why he made love to her. She started crying against him and he wanted to shut her up. He didn't realize he was going to end up naked with her.

His nerves have tightened up his muscles as his thoughts scurry in his head. He wonders if screwing a hermaphrodite makes him gay. He sure feels gay, because he kind of enjoyed it while it was happening. But, now that it's over, the image of her jerking off as he fucked her is lingering. What seemed kinky and exciting before now seems disturbing and wrong.

He's wondering if it's not that he has a problem with the fact that he's made love to a hermaphrodite, or if he has a problem with fact that he took advantage of an emotionally wrecked hermaphrodite whose lover recently died a violent death in her arms.

Really, the biggest problem he's having is why he got so incredibly horny out of nowhere. It was like an extremely potent aphrodisiac was running through his blood.

At least her penis and her vagina are lined up perfectly with her belly button. He wouldn't be able to live with himself if she was born with sloppily placed genitalia. He had to dump his first girlfriend because one of her nipples was half an inch higher on the breast than the other, and he just couldn't handle that.

His muscles begin to relax once he hears Sharp snoring. He lies back on the crusty old mattress, leaving Sharp's head where it is on his thigh.

He'd rather not wake her.

CHAPTER ELEVEN

The parties have grown so strong that they merge into one organism.
Cry and Jesus move closer together to investigate each other's parties. They scowl at one another from the distance. Cry thinks he is wasting his Telosians when they could be having sex, and Jesus thinks she is wasting her Telosians when they could be getting killed.
They come face to face on the line that separates the two sides of town.
"One of us has to go," Death says.
Cry nods. "Let's do it."
Jesus backs up a few steps, his hand hovering over the handle of the furry pistol in his belt.
Sex bends slowly, stretching her reptilian claws to the back of her thighs.
Before they draw their weapons, they are interrupted by the Telosians around them. Something is happening that has caught their attention:
The Telosians are now killing and fucking at the same time. An orgy of sex and death.
Cry and Jesus drop out of their attack-stances and turn away, investigating the people around them.
"It's beautiful," Cry says.

Death just grunts and nods his head.

They look at each other and their lips curl into wicked grins. Then they shake hands.

"We can do great things together, missy," Death says.

"Wonderful, magical things," she says.

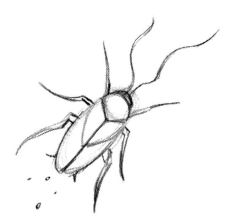

CHAPTER TWELVE

The wall of the vault collapses and the morning sun shines in. Nixx and Sharp crab-walk themselves awake, then cover their privates with wet pillows and cans of beef.

Telosians are standing in the new doorway that have just formed, laughing at them with stand-up comedy shows on their faces, slapping their knees and tumbling backwards in drunken glee.

"What the hell?" Nixx cries.

They are unsure how or why the Telosians collapsed the wall, but if these drunken idiots were able to do it he can't imagine how easy it would be for the demons.

Nixx pulls his pants and boots on. Sharp is clutching a wad of clothes against her body, she doesn't want any of them to see her hermaphrodite parts.

Nixx's shirt is somewhere in her arms, so he goes shirtless. His green face paint smudged down his neck and chest. His bandage still tight and neat across his rib cage.

He looks out across the town. It has been destroyed. The party is still raging in the streets. Television heads are slamming against each other while fucking or fighting.

Bodies are scattered through the street. Either dead or passed out from exhaustion.

Cry and Jesus have ruined the town.

CHAPTER THIRTEEN

Nixx finds Cry sunbathing nude in the back of a wagon with two sleeping (possibly dead) Telosian girls.

"What have you done?" Nixx screams.

Cry stretches her legs at him and closes her eyes.

"You've destroyed the place!"

She sighs and sits up, dangling her legs off of the edge of the wagon at him.

"Don't be such a Hoak," she says.

"What is that supposed to mean?"

"I had a beautiful time last night," she says. "I don't regret a second of it."

"You're such a disease," he says. "Why do you have to fuck everybody you come across? Why do you have to rape and molest and pervert?"

She changes the subject. "Did you have fun with Sharp last night?"

His eyebrows tighten.

"Was it cozy just the two of you in that little vault? Pressed together in the heat, sweating against each other."

Nixx doesn't say anything. He doesn't know if she's just teasing or knows he really did get intimate with Sharp last night. Maybe she saw it in her cum, maybe she can just tell by sexual intuition, or maybe in the back of her brain she can see every sexual act that happens everywhere in the world.

"Screw you," Nixx says. "Screw this whole place."

Nixx stomps away from her, kicking at the muddy road.

"Where are you going?" she calls out to him.

"Leaving," he says.

CHAPTER FOURTEEN

Sharp wanders through the bedlam of Telos in her forest skin. A drunken Telosian tries to grab her, maybe trying to rape and hurt her, but his hands fall through her skin and into her forest body. She grabs him by the belt and pulls him television first inside of her, his box head small enough to fit through her chest. But the Telosian jerks away from her before he goes all the way in. He leaps back and ogles her with a boxing show and then runs away.

After a few minutes of searching, she finds Oxy sitting on a corner with his television bride. He watches her face and she watches the television painted on his belly.

They are covered in white dust but it doesn't look like they took part in the party through the night. Oxy has been on his honeymoon. But instead of making love, he just stared into her eyes all night long.

"Looks like it was one hell of a party last night," Sharp says to him.

He raises his finger at her like Battle Johnny used to.

She goes around to his front and faces him from over his wife's shoulder.

"Did you see where Nixx went?" Sharp asks him.

"Left town," Oxy says.

"That's impossible," she says. "I was just with him thirty

minutes ago."

"Told me he was leaving," he says. "Not five minutes ago."

Sharp scans the street, squints her eyes at the end of the road in the distance. She can't see anything through the dizzy mob.

CHAPTER FIFTEEN

Nixx outside of town:

He still couldn't find his shirt when he went back to the vault, but he did get some supplies, his Hoak bow, and wrapped a quiver of arrows across his chest.

He goes west, into the changing landscape.

Today, the landscape has a cemetery theme. There are tombstones stretching as far west as he can see. Some are small wooden crosses, some are large stone angels. From monuments ten feet tall, to little stone slabs on the ground.

A mile of walking and Nixx looks back. He can hardly see Telos anymore. Just miles of cemetery in every direction. He doesn't know where he's going.

Maybe this is the end of the world, he thinks. Maybe instead of just ending it is this repetitive landscape continuing on for infinity.

That would be hell for Nixx. The cemetery is already driving him crazy because the tombstones aren't placed evenly apart from each other. It disgusts him that they aren't identical in size and shape.

The graves end after an hour and there is a large desert landscape stretching to the horizon. It is empty of bush and cactus, but there are corpses everywhere.

Black sun-dried corpses.

He approaches one of them: a goblin. They are all dead. The black goblins have died out on their own. Like a virus without a host to feed from.

Kneeling down, the crispy skeletal face is shriveled, lips dried back to reveal cracked glass teeth.

He jumps up and stomps on the creature's chest. Its rib cage crumbles under his foot and black dust rises from the body.

When the dust settles, he notices something inside of it. Something round.

He pulls the object out of the body and wipes the soot away. It is a snow globe. He shakes it and then watches as flakes of snow fall down on a cabin in the woods.

His eyes go from the globe to the corpse, pondering the globe's origin. Then he approaches another dead goblin and kicks its chest in.

"Shit," he says to the body, as he finds another strange object within: a kaleidoscope.

He picks it up and looks through the eyehole, twisting the tube for a psychedelic array of colors.

For hours, Nixx continues smashing corpses and finding little treasures inside of their bodies.

He finds: a baseball, a leather glove, a Tonka truck, a hockey mask, a bag of circus peanuts, a 2-liter of Crystal Pepsi, a teenaged girl's half-written diary, a box of staples, a glass eye, a Klingon knife (a.k.a. tajtIq), an Easter egg, a collector's edition DVD of "Cyborg" starring Jean-Claude Van Damme, a rubber band ball, a pack of GPC menthol cigarettes, an iron kitten, Cobra Commander, a rubber hand, and a shark tooth necklace.

Nixx gives up after that, but not before organizing them

into neat rows and columns. Four items by four items. He has two items leftover. The only thing of use is the strange-shaped knife, so he puts that in his belt. He doesn't need the rubber band ball. It doesn't fit in his configuration and keeps rolling around. He puts that one back in the goblin corpse he found it in, then heads back to town.

He's got to let the others know that it's safe to leave Telos.

CHAPTER SIXTEEN

Before Nixx makes it back to town, he sees a crowd of Telosians in the cemetery landscape huddled together like football players. When they notice him, they spread out, blocking him from reentering Telos.

"Shit," he says out of the side of his mouth. There's about twenty of them. They are carrying axes and pitchforks and butcher knifes. He backs away slowly with his arms raised. They slowly close in on him. Then they charge.

Nixx turns to run, but two of them have already gotten behind him. He pulls out an arrow and fires it at a charging Telosian. It hits him perfectly in the center of his chest, but he keeps staggering forward. They are extremely determined to kill him.

"Fucking Cry," Nixx screams as he fires another arrow, hitting a Telosian in the thigh.

He groans at himself for that one. It was not fired perfectly even. These Telosians are scrambling around him in such a disorganized manner that he doesn't think he can fire an arrow at any of them straight and even, so he decides not to use his last arrow.

Instead, Nixx pulls the klingon knife from his belt and points it at them as they close in on him.

He tries to calculate the right order in which to cut them, and how he should cut them. The best thing to do would be to slice their throats; cut the jugular at a perfect 90 degree angle. It must be 3.2 inches long and 1.5 centimeters deep. But he doesn't know who should go first. Perhaps if he arranges them by height . . .

A sledgehammer strikes him in the hip and he crumbles to the ground. He cries out but is happy that the Telosian hit him in the direct center of the hip. He respects that.

Another Telosian strikes him with a pitchfork sloppily, and cuts a messy hole on his arm.

Nixx's eyebrows curl angry. That is going to leave an uneven scar.

"That's it!" Nixx cries, and lunges at the pitchfork Telosian.

He stabs him four times in the chest, the holes creating a perfect square. He rolls away from him with four revolutions, and stabs another Telosian in the centers of his feet. Then jerks on the cable dangling from the back of his television head and breaks his neck.

Examining his two victims, it seems that they are both the thinnest of the group. He has decided to kill them in order of weight, from lightest to heaviest.

"Here we go," he says, and charges them.

He catches the axe of one Telosian and rips it out of his hands, but doesn't kill him because he's one of the fatter ones. Instead, he cuts the throat of a tall dangly Telosian who was tripping over his own television chord.

But he doesn't know who to attack next. There is an average-sized man and a short fat man. He can't tell which one weighs more. If only he had a scale . . .

While he's touching his finger to his chin to calculate this, an axe swings at his face and cuts the finger off.

"Son of a bitch . . ." he screams, staring at his missing finger, blood squirting out of the stump.

Now he has only nine fingers. He screams at them, "mother fucker," as he cuts off the same finger on the other hand to even things out.

After it is severed, he measures the stumps and sees that the axed finger was cut halfway between the joints and he cut his other finger off at the knuckle.

"Damn," he grumbles as he brings the klingon knife to the other stump.

A sledgehammer breaks through his kneecap sideways and he drops to the ground.

The Telosians crowd around him.

He stares up at the Telosian with the sledgehammer and begs him to smash his other kneecap in the same way . . .

CHAPTER SEVENTEEN

The party is dying down in Telos. Most of the living citizens have vanished.

Cry wanders through the wreckage seeking new people to fuck, but there's nobody in sight.

She hunts through the streets until she finds Random lying in some shade on the side of the road. She scratches her chin. He will have to do for now.

"It's your turn," she tells him.

He squints up at her. Her lizard flesh glistens in the sunlight.

"I can't take anymore," Random says.

"It's time to lose your virginity," she tells him.

"I've already lost my virginity," he says. "I've been fucking whores all night long. I'm beat."

"Not anally," she says.

He jerks upright when he sees her attaching a strap-on to her crotch. Instead of a dildo, the strap-on is a greasy metal millipede squirming through the air at him.

"No fucking way!" Random shrieks, crawling backwards.

She slams his face into the hard dirt and rips his pants down.

"Yes," she whispers into his ear and grips him by the

love handles.

The millipede crawls across Random's butt cheeks, goo drips into his crack, but it does not enter his asshole.

Cry doesn't lead it inside, her attention has been grabbed away . . .

She pulls up Random's pants and steps into the street, facing the armed and angry Telosian mob.

They have Nixx's body draped over their shoulders. Two broken legs and a broken skull. His blood leaks across their television screens.

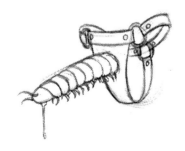

CHAPTER EIGHTEEN

Death and a few of his thugs stagger out of the saloon between Cry and the mob. He doesn't see the Telosians as he pukes on a corpse and then chugs a bottle of whiskey.

"What a night," he grunts at Sex.

She points at the Telosians down the road and he straightens up. They walk down the street. Cry is angry it has come to this, but Jesus is drunk with excitement.

The three horror show Telosians go with them. Random runs off to find Oxy and Sharp.

When they get to the mob, Jesus offers to do the translating. He's the only one who actually knows how to communicate with them, or so he says.

"They want us out of town," he drools at Cry, hardly able to stay standing.

"I'm not leaving," she says.

Jesus stares at the leader of the Telosian mob, a large farmer with The Dukes of Hazard playing on his face. It's like he can communicate with them through his eyes.

"They won't let us stay," he says. "We can either leave or they will fight us to the death."

"I want them alive," Cry says.

The metal millipede strapped to her crotch fizzle-waves

through the air at them like an electric eel.

"Either way you lose." Jesus chuckles.

Cry spits.

"If I have to kill them all I will," she says. "I'm sure there'll be plenty of cowards and wounded left when we're done."

"Just go," Nixx groans. He is still alive.

"It's safe to leave," he continues, hacking up blood. "The creatures have died. I saw them, out in the desert. They're all dried out."

Cry pretends she didn't hear him.

"Fuck it, I'm staying," she says, whipping her blade out of her thigh and slicing the Dukes of Hazard Telosian in half.

CHAPTER NINETEEN

Random, Sharp, and Oxy with his television bride arrive to a battle in the streets. They take cover behind some dead horses and watch Cry slicing up the mob of Telosians like fruit.

Death goes to draw his furry pistol but it is no longer in his belt. He looks down.

"Where the hell did it go?"

He examines his holsters and digs through his pockets. Not sure what happened to all of his guns.

A man with Friday The 13th Part Eight: Jason Takes Manhattan playing on his face comes at Jesus with an axe. Death just pukes on him and the man backs away.

The three horror show Telosians fight against their people to protect their leader, shooting into the mob with their remote controls, but are soon chopped down by the crowd.

Jesus stumbles to the side of the road and looks under a dead pig for some kind of weapon, then passes out in the mud.

Reinforcements come out of the woodwork.

The surviving Telosians see the mob fighting back against Sex and Death, and they join in. There are now more than a hundred television people coming after Cry.

"Get Jesus out of here!" she screams at Sharp and Random.

They come out of hiding and help Death to his feet.

"Take him outside of town," she says, "I'll hold them back."

Random and Sharp drag the drunken gunslinger out of the battle as Cry cuts through the citizens like a samurai. Her metal millipede dangling between her legs, her stegosaurus spikes covered in blood.

Oxy forces his wife to walk backwards behind the others, so he can watch the rest of The Fall Guy as they leave town.

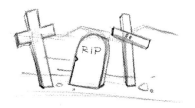

CHAPTER TWENTY

Dragging Death through the cemetery landscape:
"Where the heck are we supposed to go?" Random asks. "There's nothing out here."
"Let's circle the town north," Sharp says. "There's got to be someplace safe."

About half a mile north of the town, they see a large structure in the distance.
"What's that?" Random asks.
"Could be something," Sharp says.
They wipe ants and dirty sweat from their foreheads as they head towards the building.
"It's some kind of factory," Sharp says. "A paper mill maybe."
"There's no industry this far west," Random says. "It's probably just a barn."

The building is three stories and made of gray brick, painted with splotches of tar. The windows are barred. A loud humming emanates from within.
There's also a pond-sized dish on the roof of the structure, like a satellite dish. Sharp thinks the building is wearing a big shiny sombrero.

Random drops Jesus and opens the rusty iron door. Inside, there are churgling machines piled all the way to the roof like a metal ice cream sundae.

Cry dashes down the dirt trail, picking up dust like horse hooves. She's fatigued and covered in blood. It isn't her blood. Her cheeks are black from all the televisions exploding in her face.

She picks up Jesus and pulls him through the door.

"They're coming this way," she says. "We need to seal this place up."

Before Random enters, he sees a horde of television heads stampeding his way. There are now twice as many as before, smashing down the gravestones and cemetery crosses as they charge.

CHAPTER TWENTY-ONE

Random and Cry push heavy broken down engines and machine parts in front of the iron door, as Sharp covers the windows with sheets of steel.

Oxy just sits in the corner watching Martin on his wife's face.

"What is this place?" Sharp asks, staring across the maze of equipment.

"It's the color mill," Cry says.

Sharp jumps down from a ladder.

"Look," Cry steps over to a collection of levers in the center of the room.

She pulls one lever back and everything they see drowns in a green hue. Then she pushes the lever back in place and pulls a different lever and everything becomes a fog of yellow.

"This is where the world's color comes from," Cry says.

Random backs away from the iron door as the Telosians arrive.

"What are you talking about?" he asks. "This place generates color?"

"Yes," Cry says. "These machines create it and reflect it off the sun for the entire world."

"Have they been here since the beginning of time?"

Sharp asks.

"No," Cry says. "Color was invented about a century ago. This place was originally in the far east but people kept screwing with the color balance. They had to move it to a place far away. I had no idea it was in Telos."

"What was the world like before color?" Sharp asks.

"It was all grays."

"Gray isn't a color?"

Cry shakes her head and tries to balance the colors out.

"Crap," she mumbles. "I forgot where they were."

She fidgets with the color balances but can't seem to get it right. There seems to be too much yellow in the world, but when she dims the yellow all the colors seem weak and bland. Not colorful anymore.

"Fuck it," she says, and wanders away.

Sharp peaks at the Telosians through the window as they bang on the door with hammers and axes and torches.

"Are they going to burn us out?" she asks Cry.

Cry says, "They wouldn't dare."

CHAPTER TWENTY-TWO

The Telosians stop banging against the wall for awhile and it gets quiet. Just the white noise of a hundred different television shows playing at once.

There is a thunderstorm over the forest in Sharp's skin. Random sticks his hand in her back to get a drink of water when she isn't looking but gets a jolt of lighting in his palm.

"What was that?" Sharp asks.

Random shrugs at her. His hand in his pocket, tears dripping from his eyes.

The silence outside doesn't last very long. It ends with an eruption of screams and agonizing groans.

Sharp looks out of the window.

"It's Nixx," she says. "He's still alive."

Nixx has been crucified with barbed wire to one of the large crosses in the graveyard outside. Their leader is a Telosian in a preacher's cassock with an emergency broadcast system alert on his screen. He wraps the barbed wire around Nixx's naked body and the cross, cocooning him in it.

Another Telosian with a 70's family sitcom on his face stabs him with a rusted screwdriver between his ribs. He shrieks with every stab.

"Let me see." Cry pushes Sharp out of the way. She watches as they torture the pathetic Hoak.

The emergency broadcast system Telosian wraps the barbed wire around Nixx's scrotum and then begins yanking the wire like he's trying to rip off his testicles. Nixx's cries pierce the eardrums of Sharp and Random. They grind their teeth and clench their fists at the noise.

"Open the door," Sex tells them. "I'm going to kill every one of those fuckers."

Random grabs her from the behind, his hands carefully between the razor-sharp blades on her spine.

"You can't," he says. "You're going to get us all killed."

"We're all going to die anyway," she says.

"Not if we can hold them off until Jesus sobers up," Sharp says, in front of Cry, pushing on her chest.

"He drank enough to kill a man," Cry says. "He'll be too hungover to fight for days. We won't last that long."

"When it comes to killing, he's miraculous," Sharp says. "Even hungover he could take them all himself."

The lizard woman blows air at Sharp.

"Nixx is going to die anyway," Random says.

Cry jerks out of their grip, cutting Random's arm with her stegosaurus spikes. He freezes with his mouth wide open as he sees blood gushing out of him. She pretends she doesn't know she cut him and sits down on an oiled engine by the color controls.

She pushes the red lever all the way up to show the world how angry she is.

"Besides," Sharp says, "they'll stop torturing Nixx once they realize we aren't coming out there to stop them."

CHAPTER TWENTY-THREE

Five hours pass, the sun goes down, and Nixx is still scream-ing out there. His voice has gotten rough but he's yelling out for mercy. They have been cutting off pieces of him. His fingers, the tips of his elf ears, his nose and lower lip.

Emergency Broadcast System Face seems to enjoy cutting him. Perhaps his wife or daughter was raped and killed during the party last night. This is his bittersweet revenge, and he wants to make it last.

Inside the color mill, everyone has tuned out the Hoak's screams. The only light inside comes from the Telosian girl's face.

Random has passed out. Sharp is trying to sleep, but the thunderstorm in her forest skin is cold and keeps her awake.

Cry gets bored and masturbates onto Oxy while he watches Hogan's Heroes. He doesn't seem to realize the rep-tilian woman behind him, not even when she squirts it into his sideburns.

She frowns at the back of his head for not paying at-tention, then leans down to watch his wife's face from over his shoulder.

He laughs hysterically at the concentration camp sitcom but Cry doesn't get any of the jokes. She doesn't know why some people on the show are heil-Hitlering and other people on the show are prisoners. The Telosian's naked body is much more interesting to Cry than the show.

The woman's face turns to a crime investigation show and she begins struggling to free herself from the ropes.

"Damn it," Oxy says, and turns a knob on her face to change it back to Hogan's Heroes.

She stops struggling and relaxes.

Cry flicks her claws at the hermaphrodite's thick head and strolls away.

CHAPTER TWENTY-FOUR

Jesus wakes at the crack of dawn and pukes bile all over Random's wedding shoes.

Random wakes up and almost kicks Death in the face before he realizes who is puking on him. The boy decides to ignore the fact that he's being puked on for awhile and daydreams about the world before his wedding day.

Times were easygoing in his old life; he didn't have to worry about demon plagues or angry television mobs or getting raped in the ass by a strange tattooed woman. In some ways he feels relieved to be free of the pressures of his family and Typi and her family. They all had plans for him. Plans he didn't want for himself.

If he survives this ordeal he thinks he'll go back east if it really is safe. Look for survivors. There's got to be some out there somewhere. Maybe he'll be able to find a woman who doesn't have a television for a head or metal spikes growing down her spine.

After Death finishes vomiting, he cleans his mouth on Random's pant leg and crawls across the floor searching for his gun.

Random pulls himself to his feet and shakes the goop from his shoes. Oxy is still watching his wife's face. She tries to go to sleep on him, but he won't let her, smacks the side of her head when her screen goes fuzzy on him.

Cry is coiled around the color generator, fast asleep. The world isn't red anymore, so she must have balanced out the colors during the night.

Sharp is lying on the ground with her arm over her eyes.

Out the window:

Random sees Nixx out there, dazed and groaning. He's a bloody mess. Mostly dead, but Emergency Broadcast System Face keeps him alive so he can torture him more.

Nixx isn't crucified on a cemetery cross anymore. He's been barb-wired to something else. A large metal spiral thing.

The landscape changed again overnight. It's no longer a cemetery theme. Now it is a drill farm theme. Random gazes out to see the drill farms are just now appearing out of the soil, solidifying from gases that drift out of the clouds.

There are small shacks everywhere filled with electric drills. From handheld drills to giant construction drills that can burrow a hole a mile into the earth.

The Telosians leap out of the dirt with the appearance of the drill farms. Emergency Broadcast System Face hands out drills to the army. Four of the drills are as big as a man. They each require two men to operate them.

These large electric drills turn on as they advance the color mill and loud buzz-grinding noises fill the morning air.

CHAPTER TWENTY-FIVE

Cry wakes up to the buzz-grinding noise. Holes are being drilled into the walls around them.

She stretches herself awake and frowns at the wrecking crew. Licks her black puffy lips and gets to her feet.

"Time to kill," she says, squeezing Death's shoulders.

Oxy's eyes red and swollen, watching infomercials. He doesn't even know what's going on.

Random climbs a ladder along the side of the machine towards the rafters of the building, but Sharp decides to stay with the others in case she's needed.

Death digs through the pile of metal junk, looking for something he can fight with.

"Here," Cry says, handing Sharp and Jesus a couple of lead pipes.

Jesus looks at it like it's from outer space.

The walls are turning into Swiss cheese around them. Sharp attempts to jam a drill with her lead pipe, but the drill keeps churning.

"Where the hell's my gun?" Death says, looking around at his feet.

"You lost it yesterday," Cry says. "Make due with what you got."

Death grumbles at her.

Cracking noises from above.

Cry looks up.

She sees Random is all the way up near the ceiling, trying to balance on a jungle-gym of aluminum beams dangling from the ceiling by thin wires. The wires are breaking one by one.

"What are you doing up there?" Cry screams at him. "That won't hold your weight."

But Random is too terrified to move. His arms are wrapped around the bar, holding tightly for dear life.

Another cable breaks and the mesh of beams swings out, Random dangling upside-down, held up by a single wire.

"Don't move," Cry yells. "I'll come get you."

But before she gets to the ladder, the last cable snaps and Random falls. His body breaks against black machinery, then gets chewed into it. He doesn't scream. Just whines a little. Then he's already dead.

The aluminum beams rain onto the color generator, landing in the chains and gears. The machine grinds to a halt and a metal tinkle-noise crickets as smoke fills the room.

"It's going to explode," Cry says, waving Sharp and Jesus back.

But it doesn't exactly explode. It just falls apart. The machine becomes an avalanche of parts that rain down on them, filling the color mill with mounds of junk.

And when it's over, all the color vanishes from the world.

CHAPTER TWENTY-SIX

Everything in shades of gray:

Two holes break open in the front of the mill, bigger than doors. And the Telosian mob floods in.

They come at Cry with electric drills and axes, but stumble over all the metal junk. She's able to cut them down with her blade one at a time.

But she's soon overwhelmed by them. They come at her from all sides.

Sharp tries to fight off the Telosians with her lead pipe, but there are too many of them. She retreats behind a large mound of metal scraps where Oxy is sitting. He raises the volume on his wife's head. With all this racket around him he can hardly hear his program. It's bad enough that everything's in black and white. Now NASCAR racing is on and he'll be damned if he misses a second of it.

Death is doing just fine with his lead pipe. It took a few kills to get used to it, but now he's breaking heads and impaling chests left and right. But those little drills move too fast for him. He keeps getting drilled in the sides and back by the little Telosians that creep up on him.

A hole pops open on Jesus' chest. Something has flown right through his body. It makes him smile. Somebody has just shot him with his furry gun.

He looks up to see his gun is in the possession of a Telosian with Family Matters playing on his face. Carl Winslow and Steve Urkel are doing a dance in a living room together, as Death approaches. Two more bullets are fired into his chest before Jesus is able to grab the Telosian's arm and rip it out of the socket.

He takes the furry pistol out of the television man's hand and shoots Steve Urkel in the face.

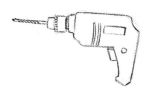

CHAPTER TWENTY-SEVEN

Cry's blade is knocked away from her by a Desperate House-wives-faced Telosian man. Then he laughs at her with a McDonald's commercial, pointing his two-handed drill at her chest.

He lunges at her, but Cry dodges to the side and changes his channel to Scooby Doo. While he's disoriented, Cry slams his neck into a spike on her upper back and blood splashes across the metal junkyard.

Now that Death has his gun, he showers the Telosians with needle-like bullets. Corpses pile up around him.

Cry backflips and her stegosaurus blades cut a Telosian in half while she's in midair. Trying to find her sword, she has to fight with the spikes on her back. Flipping and cartwheeling into attackers, lunging at them back-first.

Sharp just stands back and watches as the mill becomes drenched with dark gray blood. Smashed televisions piled up. Some of them are still partially alive with sparkling fuzz on their faces. Others have shattered screens, revealing bloody skulls within.

CHAPTER TWENTY-EIGHT

Cry smashes a young Telosian man against a wall back-first and impales him on her spikes. But when she steps forward, the boy is still attached to her back. She shakes him and pushes at him, but he's stuck. The spikes have hooked him in good.

And he's still alive, wiggling on her as she kicks other Telosians back.

Death shoots at her attackers but one gets through and drills her in the stomach. She cries out and pushes him away. Bullets tear through his television before he can strike again.

Cry sees the end of her blade sticking out of a pile of engine parts and she pulls herself toward it. But before she can reach, the boy on her back stabs a two-handed drill through the back of her chest, just below the collarbone. Then turns it on.

She thrashes around as the metal twists and grinds against her bones. She reaches around to the boy on her back and rips his throat out with her reptile claws.

The drill stops. It is still inside of her and the boy is still on her back. She looks down. Her chest has been shredded, but she's happy to see that her both of her breasts are okay.

As she sighs with relief, her body goes limp and she falls through a hole in the wall.

"Cry!" Sharp screams.

The hermaphrodite raises her lead pipe like a baseball bat at a Telosian that charges her with two cleavers and a haunting episode of The Little Rascals playing on his screen. After seeing Cry's death, she puts all her anger and passion into the swing, but the television man ducks out of the way.

He brings both of his cleavers together inside of her neck and her head pops off. It disappears into the thunderstorm raging inside of her forest skin.

CHAPTER TWENTY-NINE

With Cry out of the way, the Telosians are really able to pile in and swarm Jesus.

He shoots them full of needles like he's a sewing machine. But he doesn't see Little Rascals Face coming at him from behind with his cleavers. The Telosian chops his arm off just below the elbow and the hand flies across the room with the furry pistol still attached. He punches Little Rascals Face in the stomach and dives over a few of his friends to reclaim his severed arm.

With his other hand, he takes the furry pistol and fires into television faces. Spinning in a circle like a merry-go-round, with his only arm outstretched, he cuts down the mob with bullets as they come at him from all directions.

An axe is thrown from across the room and chops deep into his shoulder. He can't move his gun arm with the axe in there, so he pushes it out with his bloody stump. The axe falls out of his shoulder, but it takes his good arm with it.

Standing there, armless, in the circle of Telosians. Death gets angry. He yells at the top of his lungs as the television people close in on him.

But he doesn't give in. He directs his anger into his legs and kicks Little Rascals Face in the chest. His foot goes all the way through his body.

The Telosians pause.

They examine Death's leg and find the Little Rascals Face's heart is smeared across the bottom of his boot.

The Telosian drops to the metal floor.

Jesus screams again and knocks a television set off of one of their necks. Kicks another through the stomach. Breaks two of their faces.

One of the two-man drills swings at him from behind, and slices through both of his legs. They cut through at the thighs and he folds in half.

The Telosians cheer at his limbless body, but their cheers are cut short as Death grabs the furry pistol with his teeth and fires at them with his tongue. His torso leaps off of the ground and flips through the air at them, spraying holes into them.

Until his torso is impaled onto an enormous drill that poking through one of the walls. He looks over his shoulder, clinging desperately to the furry pistol in his mouth, and sees Emergency Broadcast System Face enter the mill, carrying his bible.

Death's eyes roll into the back of his head as he inches down the shaft of the drill.

CHAPTER THIRTY

The last dozen Telosians, led by Emergency Broadcast System Face, march up behind Oxy.

He's still watching television. His eyes are wide open and bloodshot. A big clown smile is frozen on his face as he sits three inches away from his wife's screen while it plays "Road House" starring Patrick Fucking Swayze.

The Telosian girl switches her channel to Mork and Mindy, snapping Oxy out of his trance. He hears Emergency Broadcast System Face and stands up.

Looking around the room, he notices that he's the only one left. All his friends are dead. He giggles at the idea.

He picks up his wife and hugs her close to him as the mob moves in, their weapons raised over their heads.

Oxy chuckles, then waves them goodbye.

Before they're able to strike, Oxy drops down into Sharp's forest skin with a wide smile across his face, pulling his Telosian bride down in there with him.

Emergency Broadcast System Face steps towards the headless body-shaped forest and looks down into it.

Holes open up on his chest and he drops to the floor.

The other Telosians scowl at his dead body with their

Twilight Zone faces, then turn around to see Death stuck to the drill on the wall. He's regained consciousness, the fuzzy gun aimed at them from his mouth.

Bullets tear through them before they can jump for cover.

CHAPTER THIRTY-ONE

Cry is still alive. She's outside staggering after the surviving wounded Telosians like a zombie. The young man is no longer attached to her back, but his drill is still inside of her collarbone. When she catches them she wrestles their weapons away and then fucks them to death.

Nixx watches her from his crucified position. He is also still alive. Just barely. Most of his skin is missing from his body. Most of his body parts are missing.

His intestines have spilled out of his belly. Some of them caught on the barbed wire, some of them in the mud. Bugs are getting into them. The sun is drying them out like beef jerky.

Cry doesn't cut him down. Busy raping and killing. She warps her legs around a man's neck and grinds her cunt against his voice box until he suffocates to death.

Then she catches another Telosian and forces him to give her oral sex with his television tongue. It gets him excited enough for her to fuck him. While she's pumping him, the drill bouncing in her chest, she breaks open the box of his television face. She takes it apart piece by piece until his bloody human head is exposed, gasping for life. Before he's able to die, she fucks his face, forces him to give her oral again. And he dies in her crotch just when she reaches orgasm, crushing his skull between her thighs.

The last Telosian she can find is crawling through the desert, riddled with holes. She flips him over on his back and sits on him like a saddle.

But she doesn't rape him. She's too tired.

Instead, she watches the pictures moving on his face. It is a Japanese movie about a man covered in metal, coming after a woman with a drill for a penis.

For the first time, television has got Cry's attention.

She lies down on top of him and rests her chin on the edge of his head, thoroughly enjoying his program.

CHAPTER THIRTY-TWO

It is not black and white where Oxy has gone. His new world is full color.

But he doesn't seem to notice. He's in too much pain. Lying in the wet forest with a broken leg and his wife's smoking face in his lap.

She didn't survive the fall. Her head cracked open against a tree on the way down.

Oxy cries out at this forest world within Sharp, for taking his beloved away from him. It echoes out of Sharp's skin and fills the color mill.

He holds her body tight to him and curses himself. He wishes it would have been his head that cracked open against the tree. Not his love's.

CHAPTER THIRTY-THREE

Nixx opens his eyes to Cry sitting cross-legged before him.

"Is this what you saw?" Nixx asks, his voice crusty and weak. "When you saw my death, did you know I would die this way?"

She lowers her eyes.

"Why didn't you tell me?" he says. "You should have known I wouldn't want to die like this. I would rather have killed myself before getting captured. How could you let me suffer for so many hours?"

She licks her chin at him.

"I'm sorry," she says. "I was just teasing you before. I had no idea how you were going to die. I just wanted you to live your life to the fullest with me."

He wheezes at her and smiles. The smile cracks the skinless tissue that has scabbed across his face.

"Kill me," he says. "It's taking forever for me to die."

Cry doesn't answer him. They both know she owes it to him. She pulls the drill out of her back and climbs his body using the barbed wire as a ladder.

He dies before she gets a chance to drill a hole through his heart, but she does it anyway, for him.

She kisses him on the cheek and closes his crunchy eyelids.

CHAPTER THIRTY-FOUR

Cry finds Death alone in the color mill, gazing proudly over a job well done.

"You're a wreck," Cry says to his limbless body.

He's managed to wiggle himself off of the drill in the wall and now lies upright in a pile of corpses.

"Oh, I'll be fine," Death says.

"You've been completely dismembered," Cry says.

"Not completely," he replies.

She notices a bulge rising in his pants and a big smile flashes across her face. He chuckles out of the side of his mouth at her.

She claps her hands together and mounts him.

Fucking on top of televisions and dead flesh:

"We've killed the whole town," Cry says, twirling her hair and staring off into space. "We'll have to find another one."

Jesus finds it difficult to fuck her without any arms or legs.

She casually bounces on top of him. "We make a good team."

"We should work together more often," he says.

"Heck yeah!" she says like a cheerleader.

She leans in and starts pounding him hard.

"The world is our play thing," she whispers into his ear.

CHAPTER THIRTY-FIVE

Oxy finishes burying his wife and creates a heart out of stones on the top of her grave. He kisses the center of the heart and wipes a tear from his eye.

He limps through the forest for hours, not sure if he's in a real world or just Sharp's clothes. Eventually he comes to a road and follows it north. There are signs at a conjunction that explain where the roads are going. The sign that points east reads "Gneirwil." The sign that points south reads "Telos." And the sign that points north reads "Dargoth Castle."

He decides to go east.

While limping down the dirt road, he twists some crunchies out of a sideburn and smells his fingers.

They smell like vagina. He knows what vaginas smell like. He has one himself. But he doesn't usually rub his sideburns after he masturbates it.

He tastes his fingers and nods. It's vagina alright. But not his . . .

His mind gets dizzy and then everything goes black.

A vision appears in his head. He sees Cry and Jesus in the not too distant future. Jesus is just a torso and Cry pushes him in a wheelbarrow. They are traveling west, away from Telos towards the end of the world. They discover there are more towns out that way, civilizations and peoples that are even stranger than the Telosians.

He sees them laughing and happy, smiling with glee in these new lands.

There are more places that will be able to experience their beauty.

More people that are in dire need of sex and death.

ABOUT THE AUTHOR

Carlton Mellick III is one of the leading authors in the new BIZARRO genre uprising. In only a few short years, his surreal counterculture novels have drawn an international cult following despite the fact that they have been shunned by most libraries and corporate bookstores. His short stories have appeared in over 100 publications, including The Year's Best Fantasy and Horror 16. He lives in Portland, OR, where he daydreams about the chick who used to play Punky Brewster.

Visit him online at: WWW.AVANTPUNK.COM

ABOUT THE ARTIST

Ed Mironiuk is an art whore that draws smart sexy ladies that could kick your ass. And when I say your ass I actually mean mine. You can see lots of his work in magazines, galleries and other junk like that. You can also check out more of his illustrations, buy swag, get useless info, or contact him about commisioning artwork at:

WWW.EDMIRONIUK.COM

BIZARRO

A new genre of film and literature.

For eons, people have been going into bookstores and video stores looking for the weird stuff. To them, "weird stuff" is a genre, just like horror or science-fiction. But it has never been given an official name before. Until now.

Bizarro directors: David Lynch, Alexandro Jodorowsky, Brothers Quay, Jan Svankmajer, Takashi Miike, Shinya Tsukamoto, Lloyd Kaufman, John Waters, among others.

Bizarro authors: Steve Aylett (steveaylett.com), Kenji Siratori (kenjisiratori.com), Carlton Mellick III (avantpunk.com), Chris Genoa (chrisgenoa.com), D. Harlan Wilson (dharlanwilson.com), Andre Duza, (houseofduza.com), Jeremy Robert Johnson (jeremyrobertjohnson.com), John Edward Lawson (johnlawson.org), Kevin L. Donihe, Mike Philbin, Alyssa Sturgill, among others.

Bizarro publishers: Raw Dog Screaming Press, Afterbirth Books, Eraserhead Press, Skull Vomit Press, among others.

Coming in 2006: www.bizarrogenre.org

Books by Carlton Mellick III
www.AVANTPUNK.com

As an underground author, Carlton Mellick III's books can only be special ordered at local bookstores or purchased through online retailers such as www.amazon.com. If you'd like this to change, please ask your bookstores and libraries to carry future CM3 books.

"this generation's Vonnegut" - Vincent W. Sakowski

Satan
Satan
Burger

an anti-novel
by Carlton Mellick III

TEETH and TONGUE
LANDSCAPE

a novel by
Carlton Mellick III
illustrated by
Brian Deegan

CHOOSE YOUR OWN MIND-FUCK FEST • 17

Choose from a bunch of different endings and shit!

OCEAN OF
LARD

by KEVIN L. DONIHE and CARLTON MELLICK III

ILLUSTRATED by TERRASA ULM

Author of RAZOR WIRE PUBIC HAIR

THE
BABY JESUS
BUTT PLUG

A FAIRY TALE

CARLTON
MELLICK
III

The
STEEL BREAKFAST ERA
a novel of the dark bizarre

Carlton Mellick III

the
Menstruating
Mall

Carlton Mellick III

Afterbirth Books

*The Menstruating
Mall*
Carlton Mellick III
$12.95

Tangerinephant
Kevin Dole 2
$10.95

*Pocket Full of Loose
Razorblades*
John Edward Lawson
$12.95

COMING SOON:

*Kafka's Uncle and Other
Strange Tales*
Bruce Taylor
AVAILABLE NOVEMBER 2005
With introduction by Brian Herbert!

- *It Came From Below the Belt*
  Bradley Sands

- *Tales from the Vinegar Wasteland*
  Ray Fracalossy

- *Deity (The Almighty's
  Adventures on Earth and Beyond)*
  Vic Mudd

- *The Hanging Gardens of Babylon*
  Gina Ranalli

*Bizarro books from bizarro
authors, presenting the surreal,
absurd, experimental, and just
plain weird.*

www.afterbirthbooks.com

Last Burn in Hell
by John Edward Lawson, 150 pgs

Kenrick Brimley is the state prison's official gigolo. From his romance with serial arsonist Leena Manasseh to his lurid angst-affair with a lesbian music diva, from his ascendance as unlikely pop icon to otherwordly encounters, the one constant truth is that he's got no clue what he's doing. As unrelenting as it is original, *Last Burn in Hell* is John Edward Lawson at his most scorching intensity, serving up sexy satire and postmodern pulp with his trademark day-glow prose.

Tempting Disaster edited by John Edward Lawson, 260 pgs

An anthology from the fringe that examines our culture's obsession with sexual taboos. Postmodernists and surrealists band together with renegade horror and sci-fi authors to re-envision what is "erotic" and what is "acceptable." By turns humorous and horrific, shocking and alluring, the authors dissect those impulses we deny in our daily lives. Includes stories by Carlton Mellick III, Michael Hemmingson, Lance Olsen & Jeffrey Thomas.

Spider Pie by Alyssa Sturgill, 104 pgs

Sturgill's debut book firmly establishes her as the *enfant terrible* of contemporary surrealism. Laden with gothic horror sensibilities, it's a one-way trip down a rabbit hole inhabited by sexual deviants and monsters, fairytale beginnings and hideous endings.

www.rawdogscreaming.com

Printed in the United States
98329LV00003B/362/A